# DIANA

# DIANA
## THE GODDESS WHO HUNTS ALONE

# CARLOS FUENTES

TRANSLATED FROM THE
SPANISH BY ALFRED MACADAM

BLOOMSBURY

First published in Great Britain 1995

Translation Copyright © 1995 by Farrar, Straus & Giroux, Inc

Originally published in Spanish under the title
*Diana o la cazadora solitaria* by Alfaguara Hispánica © 1994 by Carlos Fuentes

Translated from the Spanish by Alfred Macadam

Bloomsbury Publishing Plc, 2 Soho Square, London W1V 6HB

A CIP catalogue record for this book is
available from the British Library

ISBN 0 7475 2269 3

10 9 8 7 6 5 4 3 2 1

Printed in Great Britain by Clays Ltd, St Ives plc

# DIANA

I

No bondage is worse than the hope of happiness. God promises us a vale of tears on this earth, but at least that suffering comes eventually to an end. Eternal life is eternal bliss. Rebellious, unsatisfied, we argue with God: Don't we deserve even a taste of eternity during our passage through time? God has more tricks than a Las Vegas cardsharp. He promises us joy in the hereafter and sorrow on earth. We convince ourselves that knowing life and living it well in His vale of tears is the supreme defiance of God. Of course, if we are triumphant in our rebellion, God gets even: He denies us immortality at His side and condemns us to eternal pain.

Contrary to all logic, we ascribe logic to the Divinity. We tell ourselves, God could not be the creator of misery and suffering, human cruelty and human barbarity. We say, in any case, it was not a good God who created that but a bad God, the God of appearances, the masked God whom we can overcome only by wielding the weapons of evil that He him-

3

self forged. Sex, crime, and, above all, the imagination of evil: aren't these also the gifts of a malevolent God? So we persuade ourselves that only if we murder the usurper God will we, clean in body, mentally free, see the face of the first God, the good God.

But the great cardsharp has yet another ace up his sleeve. When we've worn out body and soul trying to reach Him, God reveals that He is only what He is not. All we can know about God is what He is not. To know what God is is something neither saints, nor mystics, nor Church Fathers know; not even God Himself knows. He'd collapse, fulminated by His own intelligence, if He knew.

Bedazzled, Saint John of the Cross is the mortal who has come closest to God's intelligence, just so he can communicate this news to us: "God is Nothing, the supreme Nothing, and to reach Him, we must travel toward the Nothing, which cannot be touched or seen or understood in human terms." And to humiliate hope, Saint John leaves us only this terrible passage: "All the being the creatures possess, compared with the infinite being of God, is nothing . . . All the beauty of the creatures, compared with God's infinite beauty, is the greatest ugliness." Perhaps Pascal, French, a saint, and a cynic, is the only thinker whose wager saves both our conscience and our concupiscence: if you wager that God exists and He doesn't, you lose nothing, but if God does exist, you win everything.

Standing between Saint John and Pascal, I give God a nominal, that is substantive, value: God is the shorthand term for what brings origins and destiny together in a single embrace. The reconciliation of these two terms has been humanity's immemorial task. To choose origins alone is at first a lyrical, then very quickly a totalitarian nostalgia. To wed oneself exclusively to destiny can be a form of fatalism or fortune-telling. Origins and destiny should be inseparable: memory and desire, the living passage in the present, the future, here and now . . . That's where I'd like to locate Diana Soren, a woman perversely touched by the Divine.

Standing between Pascal and Saint John of the Cross, I would like to create a mythic, verbal world for her that would approach the mendicant question that stretches out its hands between earth and heaven: Can we love on earth and someday deserve heaven? Instead of being penitents, flagellants, hermits, or creatures starved for life, can we fully participate in it? Can we obtain and deserve earthly fruits without sacrificing eternal life? Without begging forgiveness for having loved "not wisely but too well"?

Christian mythology, which opposes charity to the implacable judgment of the Old Testament, does not attain the beautiful ambiguity of pagan mythology. The protagonists of Christianity are always themselves, never others. They demand an act of faith, and faith, Tertullian said, is absurd: "It is true because it is incredible." But what is absurd is not necessarily ambiguous. Mary is a virgin, though she conceives. Christ rises, though He dies. But who is Prometheus, he who steals the sacred fire? Why does he exercise his freedom so as to lose it? Would he have been freer if he hadn't used it and lost it though he didn't win it either? Can freedom be conquered by a value other than freedom itself? On this earth, can we love only if we sacrifice love, if we lose the person we love though our own acts, our own failure to act?

Is something preferable to everything or nothing? That's what I asked myself when the love affair I'm going to tell about here ended. She gave me everything and took everything from me. I asked her to give me something better than everything or nothing. I asked her to give me something. That something can only be the instant in which we were, or thought we were, happy. How many times did I ask myself, Will I always be what I am now? I remember, and I write to recover the moment when she would forever be as she was that night with me. But all unique things, amatory, literary, in memory or desire, are quickly abolished by the great tide that always rolls over us like a dry flame, like a burning flood. All we have to do is leave our own skin for an instant to know that we are surrounded by an all-powerful pulsation that precedes and survives us. For that pulsation, my life or hers, our very existences are unimportant.

I love and I write to obtain an ephemeral victory over the immense and infinitely powerful mystery of what is there but does not show itself . . . I know the triumph is fleeting. On the other hand, it makes invincible my own secret power, which is to do something—this very moment—unlike anything in the rest of our lives. Imagination and language show me that, for imagination to speak and for language to imagine, the novel must not be read as it was written. This condition becomes extremely dangerous in an autobiographical text. The writer must be lavish in presenting variations on his chosen theme, multiply the reader's options, and fool style with style through constant alterations in genre and distance.

This becomes an even greater need when the protagonist is a movie actress, Diana Soren.

It's said that Luchino Visconti provoked a combination of surprise and delight in Burt Lancaster during the filming of a scene from *The Leopard* when he stuffed with silk stockings a bag supposedly filled with gold. Diana was like that: a surprise for everyone because of the incomparable smoothness of her skin, but most of all a surprise for herself, her skin surprised by her own pleasure, astonished at being desired, smooth, perfumed. Didn't she love herself, didn't she feel she deserved herself? Why did she want to be someone else? Why wasn't she comfortable in her own skin? Why?

I—and I lived with her only for two months—want to run even now to embrace her again, feel her for the last time and assure her that she could be loved with passion, but for herself, that the passion she sought did not exclude her true self . . . But the chance for that is gone. We leave a lover. We return to a woman we don't know. The eroticism of visual representation consists, precisely, in the illusion that the flesh is permanent. Like everything else in our time, visual eroticism has accelerated. Over the course of centuries, medallions and paintings were created to make up for the absence of the loved one. Photography accelerated the illusion of presence. But only cinematographic images simultaneously give us evocation and immediacy. This is how she was then but also how she is now, forever . . .

It's her image but also her voice, her movement, her undying beauty and youth. Death, the great stepmother of Eros, is both overcome and justified by this reunion with the loved one who is no longer with us, having broken the grand pact of passion: united until death, you and I, inseparable . . .

Only movies give us the real image of the person: she was this way, and even if she's acting Queen Christina she's Greta Garbo, even if she's pretending to be Catherine of Russia she's Marlene Dietrich. The Soldier Nun? But it's only Maria Félix. Literature on the other hand liberates our graphic imagination: in Thomas Mann's novella, Aschenbach dies in

Venice with the thousand faces of our imagination all in motion; in Visconti's film, he has only one face, fatal, unexchangeable, fixed, that of the actor Dirk Bogarde.

Diana, Diana Soren. Her name evoked that ancient ambiguity. Nocturnal goddess, lunar metamorphosis, full one day, waning the next, a silver fingernail in the sky the day after, eclipse and death within a few weeks ... Diana the huntress, daughter of Zeus and twin sister of Apollo, virgin followed by a retinue of nymphs but also mother with a thousand breasts in the temple at Ephesus. Diana the runner who only gives herself to the man who runs faster than she. Diana of the crossroads, called for that reason Trivia: Diana worshipped at the crossroads of Times Square, Piccadilly, the Champs Elysées ...

After all is said and done, the game of creation defeats itself. First because it takes place in time, and time is a fucking bastard. The novel takes place in 1970, when the illusions of the 1960s were doing their best not to die, assassinated but also vivified by blood. The first revolt against what our own fatal fin de siècle society would be: so brief, so illusory, so repugnant, the sixties killing their own heroes, the U.S. saturnalia devouring its offspring—Martin Luther King, the Kennedys, Jimi Hendrix, Janis Joplin, Malcolm X—and enthroning its cruel stepfathers, Nixon and Reagan.

Diana and I would play the Rip Van Winkle game: what would the old man say if he woke up after sleeping for a hundred years and found himself in the United States of 1970, with one foot on the moon and the other in the jungles of Vietnam? Poor Diana. She saved herself from waking up today and seeing a country that lost its soul in the twelve Reagan–Bush years of spurious illusions, brain-killing banalities, and sanctioned avarice. She saved herself from seeing the violence her country brought to Vietnam and Nicaragua, which boomeranged back to the sacrosanct streets of a suburbia profaned by crime. She saved herself from seeing the primary schools drowning in drugs, high schools becoming mad, gratuitous battlegrounds; she saved herself from seeing the daily random death of children murdered by pure chance when they happened to look out a window, fast-food customers machine-gunned with hamburgers still in their mouths, serial murderers, unpunished looters, ritualized corruptions because theft, fraud, murder to obtain power and glory were part—why not?—of the American Dream.

What might Diana have said, what might the solitary huntress feel, seeing the children of Nicaragua mutilated by weapons from the United States, seeing blacks kicked and their heads split by the Los Angeles police, seeing a parade of grand liars in the Iran–Contra conspiracy swearing the truth and proclaiming themselves heroes of freedom? What might she say, she who lost her child, of a country that is seriously considering sentencing child criminals to death? She would say that the 1960s ended up by going white, fading like Michael Jackson, the better to punish anyone of color. I'm writing in 1993. Before the century ends, the burning graves, the dry rivers, the swampy slums will fill up with the color of migrant Mexicans, Africans, South Americans, Algerians, of Muslims, and Jews, over and over . . .

Diana the goddess who hunts alone. This narrative, weighed down by the passions of time, defeats itself because it never reaches the ideal perfection of what can be imagined. Nor does it desire that perfection, since if language and reality were identical, the world would come to an end, the universe would no longer be perfectible, simply because it would be perfect. Literature is a wound from which flows the indispensable divorce between words and things. All our blood can flow out of that hole.

Alone at the end as we're alone at the beginning, we remember the happy moments we save from the deep latency of the world, we demand the slavery of happiness, and we only listen to the voice of the masked mystery, the invisible throb that in the end manifests itself to demand the most terrible truth, the sentence that brooks no appeal, of time on earth:

You did not know how to love. You were incapable of loving.

Now I'll tell this story to admit just how right the horrible oracle of truth was. I didn't know how to love. I was incapable of loving.

**II**

I met Diana Soren at a New Year's Eve party. Actually, it was a double celebration the architect Eduardo Terrazas staged at his house: the New Year and a reconciliation between me and my wife, Luisa Guzmán. Eduardo and I had shared a little house in Cuernavaca during 1969. I would write from Monday to Friday, then he and his girlfriend would come down from Mexico City for a weekend devoted to friends, food, and alcohol. Lots of women passed through. I had turned forty in 1968 and gone into a midlife crisis that lasted the whole year and culminated in a party I gave for my friend the American novelist William Styron in the Opera Bar on Avenida Cinco de Mayo, a tarnished but flashy leftover from Mexico's *belle époque* (supposing there really was such a thing). The Opera was down at the heels—too many domino matches and near-misses at the spittoon.

I invited all my friends to honor Styron, who had recently published *The Confessions of Nat Turner*, a very successful

11

and very provocative book. The parties most provoked were members of black organizations who said that Styron had no right to speak in the voice of a black man, Nat Turner, who in 1831 led an uprising of sixty fellow slaves, burning buildings and killing in the name of freedom until he himself was killed in a woods where he'd survived on his own for two months. Because of his insurrection, the slave laws were tightened. But because they were so tight they kindled even greater revolts. Styron recounted one—but only one—of the stations in the calvary of the United States, which is racism.

When Bill feels he's being hounded in his country, he calls me and visits Mexico, and I do the same when Mexico starts getting on my nerves, knowing I can always take refuge on Martha's Vineyard, Bill's island on the edge of the North Atlantic. Now the two of us were living in a little house I rented when I separated from Luisa Guzmán. Located in the cobblestoned neighborhood of San Angel, a separate city until recently, where families from the capital would vacation in the last century and that now survives disguised in monastic robes amid the noise and smoke of the Periférico, the beltway around the capital, and Avenida Revolución.

My neo-bachelor residence was constructed out of debris salvaged from torn-down buildings. It was designed by another Mexican architect, Caco Parra, who specializes in combining huge hacienda doors, pilasters from nationalized churches, ancient beams from the long-disappeared age of the viceroys, sacrilegious columns, and profaned altars: a complete history of how the privileged havens of the past were transformed into the civil, transitory sanctuaries of the present. Using all these elements, Parra built strange, attractive houses, so mysterious that their inhabitants could wander into their labyrinths and never be seen again.

Martha's Vineyard, on the other hand, is open to the four winds, incinerated by the sun for three months of the year and then battered by the frozen blasts of that great white whale the North Atlantic. Whenever I think of Styron holed up on his island, I imagine that Melville's Captain Ahab sailed out to kill not the whale but the ocean, Neptune himself, just as the Belgian imperialists in Conrad's *Heart of Darkness* fire their cannon not at a black enemy but at an entire continent: Africa. On Styron's island, even during the hottest months, the fog rolls in every night from the sea, as if to remind the summer that it's only a transient veil that will be torn open by the great gray cloak of a long winter. The fog comes in from the sea, over the beaches, the cliffs at Gay Head, the docks at Vineyard Haven, the lawns and the houses, until it reaches the umbilicus of the island, the melancholy inland ponds where the sea recognizes itself and dies, drowned.

In winter, the sea howls around the island but not as loudly as my guests at the Opera. I was imprudent enough to invite, willy-nilly, all my current girlfriends, making each one think she was my favorite. I loved to create situations like that: dissimulated passion, rage on the verge of augmenting passion, jealousy about to overflow like a wound to stain our blouses, our shirts, as if we were bleeding from our nipples—all this enabled me to see clearly the fragility of sex and to celebrate instead the vigor of literature.

So I invited not only my lovers to the party at the Opera but new writers like José Agustín, Parménides García Saldaña, and Gustavo Sáinz, who were fifteen years younger than I and who deserved the laurels already wilted on much older heads—mine, for instance. Totally free, uninhibited, funny, mortal enemies of solemnity, these members of the Onda movement wrote to a rock beat and were the natural stars of a party that also wanted to say to the authoritarian, murderous government of October 2, 1968: You last six years. We'll last a whole lifetime. Your saturnalia is bloody and oppressive. Ours is sensual and liberating.

Such justifications did not absolve me of the frivolity—to say nothing of the cruelty—of my erotic games. At the time I believed, despite everything, that literature, my gospel, excused everything. Others surrendered in the name of literature to drugs, alcohol, politics, even to polemics as a literary sport. I—and I wasn't alone—succumbed to love, but I retained my right to keep my distance, to manipulate, to be cruel. I was only too happy to wear the costume of Beltenebros, the Lucifer who inhabits the shining moral armor of the chivalric hero Amadis of Gaul. No sooner does Amadis lose his heroism and yield to passion than he becomes his enemy brother, Le Beau Ténébreux: Don Juan.

The Don Juan temptation is erotic but it's also literary. Don Juan endures because nothing can satisfy him (or, as the best contemporary incarnation of Don Juan grafted onto Lucifer would sing it, *I can't get no satisfaction*). It's a fact that the insatiability of the rake from Seville opens the doors of perpetual metamorphosis to him. Always desirous, always avid, he never ends, never dies: He continually transforms. He's born young, and after just a few love affairs (two or three in Tirso de Molina), he becomes old in an instant, sated but unsatisfied, an evil and cruel gentleman (in Molière). Tirso's perverse and juvenile cherub becomes the actor Louis Jouvet's mortal mask, a rationalist Gallic gargoyle who no longer believes that adolescence will last forever (he repeats, whenever reminded of death, "Let's hope it's a long way off") but who wears his own death mask. Byron, to avoid competition,

14

tames Don Juan and sits him down to have tea with his family during one of those English winters "ending in July, to recommence in August." But he gives a perverse, quasi-Argentine twist to this domestic metamorphosis. Don Juan discovers he's in love not with love but with himself, like Argentines who are bored in elevators without mirrors. Don Juan's love for Don Juan is a despotic trap—nothing less than that of love itself.

To be all that—what a dream, what an elixir—Gautier's Don Juan, Adam expelled from paradise but remembering Eve, the imprisoned memory that ties him to the perpetual quest for the lost lover and mother; Musset's Don Juan, sunk in a world of dives and whorehouses where he hopes to find the "unknown woman." He deludes himself; he's only looking for Don Juan, and even if all women look like him, none of them *is him*. But perhaps the real Don Juan, the most public because the most secretive, is Lenau's, who admits he wants to possess all women simultaneously. That is Don Juan's ultimate triumph, his most certain pleasure. To have all of them at the same time.

"Tonight I'm going to have them all. All of them."

Don Juan's pleasure depends more on disguise and movement than on ubiquity. He's like a shark: he's got to keep moving all the time so he won't sink to the bottom of the sea and drown. He moves, he moves around masked, his mask covering his larval, mutating, metamorphosing condition. He moves and changes so rapidly that his own images can't catch up with him. Neither Achilles nor the Tortoise, Don Juan is the parable of the disguised man whose disguises are always running after him. He's naked. He takes his pleasure naked. But to move, he has to dress up, disguise himself and leave behind his most recent disguise, already known, already pen-

15

etrated, before he puts on the next. In his momentary help-lessness, in his Duchampian nakedness scaling balconies and descending ladders, Don Juan is Don Juan only so he can leave his own image behind. He runs, uncatchable by any image that might want to capture him, experiencing the ve-locity of pleasure in the velocity of change, conquering all frontiers. Don Juan is the founder of the European Common Market: he has lovers in Italy, Germany, France, and Turkey, and in Spain—Mozart tells us—a thousand and three. The Machiavelli of sex, a figure disguised in order to escape the vengeance of fathers and husbands but, above all, to escape tedium ... That is how I, secretly, ridiculously, painfully, wanted to be ...

Minimal forty-year-old Don Juan of the Mexican night, I aspired as a man to that power of metamorphosis and move-ment. But most of all, I wanted it as a writer. Loving or writ-ing, nothing is more exciting or more beautiful than recognizing the struggle between the power we exercise over another person and the power the other—man or woman—exercises over us. Everything else vanishes in that ungraspable tempest of mutual attraction, of resistance that, out of lust for power or a mere instinct of survival or perhaps perversity, we put up to the attraction of another. The charm of such a struggle, obviously, is to yield to it. How? With whom? When? For how long? This is the common ground shared by sex and literature. An ashen-winged angel flies over. That dark angel, that tarnished Eros, is Don Juan, Cupid in flames, his own androgynous *putto*, who deposits on the eyelids, in the nostrils, the ears, the mouth, the anus of the loved one, on the back of the head, if necessary, the seeds of a smile, of a voice, of a glance. Of a desire. Beltenebros the melancholy whispers softly in my ear and tells me, "There can be nothing sadder than the taste of the women you will never possess, the men you lost out of fear, out of conventionality, out of dread of taking the forbidden step, out of lack of imagination, out of inability to become, as Don Juan does, someone else."

I want to be very frank in this story and keep nothing to myself. I can wound myself whenever I like. But I don't have the right to wound anyone who isn't me, unless, of course, I amorously sink into myself the dagger I end up sharing with someone else. Right here at the outset, I list the terrors that assail me. I try to justify sex with literature and literature with sex. But the writer—lover or author—ultimately disappears. If he shouts, he disintegrates. If he sighs, he's done for. You've got to be conscious of this before affirming, above all things, that life is never generous twice.

That night at the Opera Bar, in a Viscontian, which is to say *operatic*, setting, I felt I'd sunk the dagger too frequently, wounding myself more than I'd wounded the women whom I'd tried to manipulate but who, I knew only too well, could repay me in the same coin. I chose one, I earned the hatred of the rest, and Styron, Terrazas, and I left the next day for Guadalajara and the Pacific coast, where the Hotel Camino Real in Puerta Vallarta, designed by my friend, was celebrating its grand opening.

It was there I received the foreseeable lesson. One afternoon, the girl I was traveling with casually left a letter on the bed in our hotel room. She was writing to another of her boyfriends, arranging a date for New Year's Eve, which, of course, she refused to spend with me. "Writers only for a little while, because they give me brain food so I can make better love with you, darling. Besides, the oldtimers have their own kind of kicks . . . like drinking champagne all day. It just gives me heartburn. Put some sodas on ice for me, baby. Remember, if there's no Coke, I just don't celebrate . . ."

I pretended not to notice, but when I got back to Mexico City, I went to see my wife and asked her to spend New Year's Eve with me and to end a separation that had lasted almost a year. Once again, she would be my total victory over transitory loves.

# III

Luisa Guzmán had been—still was—a woman of exceptional beauty. Dark-haired, with pale, crepuscular, luminous skin that glowed brightly instead of darkening in the light of her huge black eyes, which were slanted, almost Oriental, resting above the twin continents of her high, Asiatic, tremulous cheekbones. There was a reverie in her eyes, a languor, as if while searching for herself she had been stricken with a resigned, culpable sadness. She was an actress who wanted more than the Mexican movie industry could give her. She had made her debut at the age of fifteen, an aspirant to the pantheon of Mexican film goddesses, all dark-haired like her, all tall, with sleepy eyes and the cheekbones of an immortal skull.

She never got the parts, the stories, or the directors that could have brought about the tiny miracle called stardom. She avidly searched for the best, both in film and on stage; she loved her profession so much that, paradoxically, it destroyed her. Just like Diana Soren, she made only two or three good films. Later, just to keep working, she would take any part that came along. Time and wear took away her voice, denied her starring roles, made her prematurely old; she looked for character-actor parts, opportunities to shine that no one understood because they were so eccentric.

When we met, Luisa was married and I was emerging from a failed attempt at "decent" marriage. One after another, the proper young ladies my family's status brought me into contact with would end up abandoning me, obeying their parents' ironclad rules: I wasn't rich, and even though I came from a good family, I didn't belong to a grand political or financial clan. Besides, my talent was yet to be proven. In the best of cases, writing is a risky profession, especially in Latin America: in our countries, who lives off his books?

From my amatory youth, all I had left was the taste of many young and fresh lips and, over the years, questions: What have they said? When did they lose their freshness? When will they be cracks instead of lips? I loved none of them so much as I loved a dead girlfriend burned to cinders in an air crash; there was no girl in my life with fresher lips. But her ashes were also those of the lips of another woman I was on the verge of marrying. She rejected me because I wasn't Catholic enough; I was, her parents said, an atheist and a Communist. She married a gringo with enormous feet, a belly swollen from too many beers, and a string of Texaco stations in the Midwest.

But the girlfriends were also part of an unknown sign, part of that horror I evoked at the start of my story, which consists in trying to penetrate the powerful mystery of what has yet to show itself. There is no greater melancholy than this: not knowing all the beings we might have loved, to die before we know them. My girlfriends—kissed, touched, desired, only occasionally possessed—all belonged, ultimately, to that magma of the unknown or unsaid. They all returned to the vast field of my possibility, my ignorance.

I met Luisa Guzmán before the success of my first novel. I think she loved me for myself, and I loved her for her beauty, which was obvious, and for her simplicity, which was disguised by a whirl of furs, rumors, images. More often than in her films, I had seen her in newspapers, ascending or descending airplane gangways clutching a huge plush panda. It was her trademark. An infantile image but closer to the truth than any publicity story could be.

Luisa's childhood was miserable: a father who was absent or, rather, exiled by her mother's aristocratic pride. The mother, a rebellious writer from a "good" Puebla family, always put her sexual or literary egoism before any family obligation. One day, Luisa's father, tall, Indian, coarse, found the door of his wife and daughter's home locked and he disappeared forever in the high mist and piquant scent of our mountains. Luisa, a child then, was sent to an orphanage and reemerged, an adolescent, only when her beauty and her mother's profession came into a favorable conjunction in her mother's little brain.

Damaged, Luisa came to me like a wounded bird, flying from a theater set on Sullivan Street into my waiting arms, which yearned for her, to fill a solitude that was creative but also stupid. The months of discipline and dissipation during which I had distanced myself forever from my family's social world and struggled to finish my book had left me with empty arms. She came to fill them with her passion and tenderness but also with a sadness in her captive eyes. That sadness was an early disquiet for my own joy. I finished a book; I love a woman.

It took me a long time to understand that the melancholy in Luisa's eyes was not temporary but consubstantial with them. It came, who knows, from her father's misty, spicy mountains, from the faded sadness of those Puebla houses and their inhabitants, often querulous and hypocritical, as is appropriate to that region—a hotbed of warlords and nuns, of cruelly ambitious men and cruelly devout women. But more than anything, in my wife's mestizo beauty I recognized her father's foggy, piquant mountains, where patience and goodness accumulate along with rancor and revenge.

# IV

Now Luisa and I were together again at the New Year's Eve party Eduardo Terrazas was throwing, and Luisa was more beautiful than ever—dark, tall, showing lots of cleavage in a black dress that reflected the brilliance of her teased hair, of her eyebrows and lashes, almost of her dark skin that shone like some Aztec moon, sculpted, fighting to make visible its secret interior light devoid of color; or perhaps she offered her color in a spectrum of emotions, situations, and accidents that reconciled the profound solidity and the tremendous insecurity of this woman: between those two poles, her destiny took on its own form.

She felt she was permanent, and she was. She forgave me everything; I'd always come back to her. She was the safe haven, the peaceful lagoon where I could write. She knew my truth. Literature is my real lover, and everything else—sex, politics, religion (if I had one), death (when it comes)—passes through literary experience, which is the filter of all the other experiences of my life. She knew it. She prepared and maintained the home of my writing like a perpetual flame, always waiting for me, come what may. My friends knew it, and the most generous among them, if they were friends of my lovers, would warn them: "He'll never leave Luisa. You have to understand that. On the other hand, you'll always have a friend in me."

Which is to say, the hard and fast rule for the Don Juans of all times is summed up in this Mexican adage: "Let's see if she's like chewing gum and sticks." I was no exception. They all brought their chewing gum and tried to stick, sometimes successfully, other times not. Some wives would never stand for that; others would simply pretend not to see. Luisa and I had an express pact. Even if my chewing gum stuck, I'd come back. I would always come back. That was the worst blackmail. I was always in danger of having her pay me back in the same coin. Maybe she did. Women—the best women—know how to keep secrets, unlike stereotypical gossips. The most interesting women I know never tell anyone about their sexual lives. Not even their best friends. And nothing intrigues and excites a man more than a woman who keeps secrets better than he does. But Don Juan, by definition, proclaims his triumphs, wants to have them known, wants to be envied. Luisa was secret. I—a contemptible clown, a sexual tourist—didn't deserve the loyalty, solidity, and constantly renewed faith of a woman like Luisa. That was her strength. That's why she put up with everything. That's why I was with her once again that night. She was stronger than I was.

Lots of friends were at Eduardo Terrazas's house that Feast of Saint Sylvester, December 31, 1969. José Luis Cuevas, the extraordinary artist whose painful embrace includes all the marginal, excluded visions of desire, along with his

24

wife, Berta. Fernando Benítez, my good and old friend, the great promoter of culture in the Mexican press, the novelist, the explorer of the invisible Indian Mexico, and his wife, Georgina. At the age of thirty-five, Cuevas was a wildcat whose pretense to urbane manners barely camouflaged his savage, nervous nature, for he was always on the point of pouncing on some prey as hot-blooded as he to tear it to pieces, devour it, all so he'd be left with the sensuality of being able to imagine doing it again. Was there a murderer in him sublimated by art? I always thought so, just as in Benítez—a sensualist if ever there was one, a sexist, a man who adored women but was a misogynist and hermit—there was a Franciscan monk, a Bartolomé de las Casas, redeemer of the Indians, one of those monks who came to the New World to save souls and protect bodies as soon as the conquest of Mexico was finished. It was possible to imagine him driving a BMW convertible at top speed toward Acapulco and an orgiastic weekend, but it was equally possible to see him riding a burro up some inhospitable mountain where there awaited him not lost tribes but the bacteria that was destroying his stomach, his pancreas, his intestines . . .

New Year's Eve. This passage from 1969 to 1970 was worthy of celebration because it marked the end of one decade and the beginning of a new one. But no one agrees about what that final zero means at the end of a year. Were the 1960s coming to an end and the 1970s beginning, or were the 1960s demanding one more year, a final agony of partying and crime, revolt and death, for that decade replete with major events, tangible and intangible, guts and dreams, cobblestones and memories, blood and desire: the decade of Vietnam and Martin Luther King, the Kennedy assassinations and May 1968 in Paris, the Democratic convention in Chi-

25

cago and the massacre in Tlatelolco Plaza, the death of Marilyn? A decade that seemed to be programmed for television, to fill the sterile scheduling wastelands of blank screens but leave them breathless, making miracles banal, transforming the little electronic postage stamp into our daily bread, the expected into the unexpected, the facsimile of reality that culminated, even before the 1970s had begun, in mankind's first step on the moon. Our immediate suspicion: was the flight to the moon filmed in a TV studio? Our instantaneous disenchantment: can the moon go on being our romantic Diana after a gringo leaves his shit up there?

More guests arrived. China Mendoza, journalist and writer, who had a spectacular sense of self-affirmation during the 1960s. In that decade of outrageous styles, she wore clothing she seemed to have invented on her own, not copied from a fashion magazine. That night I remember her decked out in silver glasses shaped like butterflies and a miniskirt that was actually pajamas, a pink ruffled babydoll that revealed matching panties.

Rosa, the incredibly beautiful widow of the artist Miguel Covarrubias, came with a New York art dealer who looked exactly like the actor Sydney Greenstreet—that is, he was immensely fat and old, bald, with tufts of white hair here and there, eyebrows thick as caterpillars, and liver lips. Rosa was wearing one of her golden Fortuny dresses that rolled up like a towel and unfolded like a flag proclaiming *My country is my body*. On the verge of death, Rosa Covarrubias belied her age. She, too, belonged to that pantheon of Mexican beauties, those "immortal skulls," as Diego Rivera called them when he painted Dolores del Río. How right he was. The bones of the face never grow old; they're the paradox of a death that by definition has no age, borne like the secret insignia of beauty and its price. Luisa Guzmán—I saw her walk off and go up the stairs—belonged to that race. The closer the bone was to the skin, the more beautiful the face. But the more visible was death as well. Beauty lived off its imminent dying.

Along with Rosa and Greenstreet came three English *marchands de tableaux* who stared in shock and disgust at the Mexican men embracing, slapping one another on the back, and grabbing one another by the waist. Englishmen find touching repugnant and recoil in horror at the merest brush with someone else's skin. Their ideas about climate and temperature are also singular, and one of them, the spitting image of Prime Minister Harold Wilson, recited the very lines from Byron I had just remembered: "The English winter—ending in July, / To recommence in August." He added that it was very hot and opened a window.

Terrazas had decorated his house with myriad balloons strung from the ceiling in expectation of the moment of passage from one year to another. The balloons were stamped with the logo of the 1968 Olympiad, which Terrazas himself had designed. Just as the clock was striking twelve, Berta Cuevas, to announce the new year, touched her burning cigarette to the cluster of balloons that Terrazas had bunched together to imitate the traditional twelve grapes of the celebration. She didn't know the balloons had been inflated with gas. The explosion went off like a muted earthquake and threw all of us to the floor or against the walls, swept the tables clean, turned over chairs, and knocked pictures cockeyed.

A seventeenth-century carving fell right on Greenstreet's head, and all the rest of us—Rosa, Georgina and Fernando Benítez, Cuevas and Berta, China, and I—were blind to one another, aware only of our individual selves, of our brush with death, of the instantaneous surprise of the accident, of the cancellation of all questions but one—Am I alive? Then came moans, anger, pain. We were all completely flabbergasted. We stood there with our mouths hanging open and then began to laugh as the three Englishmen, no longer so nonchalant, peered into the mirror to make certain of their existence and found their faces dotted with pieces of balloon bearing the logo of the Mexican Olympiad of 1968. They looked like three explorers suddenly transformed by the sorcery of a tribal sacrifice into priests tattooed by the very rites they'd come to exorcise. One of them— I'd recovered my senses—saved our lives by opening a window to let in a breeze that came, no doubt about it, straight from the Scottish Highlands.

Luisa saved herself and her impeccable appearance: she'd gone up to the powder room and now came back down in alarm. Just at that moment, the front door opened, and Eduardo Terrazas walked in with Diana Soren, whom he'd gone to fetch from another party.

"Are we too late?" asked our host, watching us, dazed, get up from the floor.

# V

Can you extricate yourself from one romance and get into another without hurting someone? This is just one simple example of the myriad questions you ask yourself when you suddenly realize something's going to begin at the expense of something that's going to end. She was small, blond, with boyishly cut hair, fair, pale, with blue or perhaps gray eyes, very jolly eyes, that nicely matched her dimpled cheeks. Her dress wasn't very attractive: a long Greco-Californian evening gown, which didn't suit her because it made her seem shorter than she was, like a thumbtack.

I—who else?—remembered her from her two major films. In both, Diana Soren used her adolescent physique to full advantage by dressing as a man. First she was Joan of Arc, and the armor allowed her to move with energy and fluidity, comfortable in war as she never would have been in a court of hoop skirts and white wigs, armed to fight like a soldier, dressed as a soldier. In the bonfire, she would pay dearly for

29

the privilege, accused of witchcraft but also perhaps, silently, of lesbianism and androgyny. In the only good movie she made after that, in France, she was a girl in a T-shirt and jeans running back and forth on the Champs Elysées waving her copy of the *Herald Tribune* ... Loose, free, the warrior maiden of Orléans or the vestal virgin of the Latin Quarter, adorably feminine because to get to her you had to negotiate the twists and turns of androgyny and homoeroticism. On the screen, I'd always seen Diana Soren with an unwritten subtitle: There is the love that dares not speak its name, but there is something worse, which is the love without a name. What name can I give the possible love with this pure possibility which entered the 1970 New Year's Eve party after a gas explosion and which was called Diana Soren?

I looked at her. She looked at me. Luisa looked at us looking at each other. My wife walked over to me and said point-blank, "I think we should be on our way."

"But the party hasn't even started," I protested.

"For me it's over."

"Because of the explosion? I'm fine. Look." I showed her my steady hands.

"You promised tonight to me."

"Don't be so self-centered. Look who's just walked in. We're both fans of hers."

"Forget the plural, please."

"I just want to chat with her for a while."

"Don't come home too late." She raised her eyebrow, an almost inevitable, Pavlovian, instinctive reflex in a Mexican actress.

I never went home. Seated next to Diana Soren, talking about movies, about life in Paris, discovering mutual friends, I felt I was being unfaithful and, as always, told myself that, if I wasn't being unfaithful to literature, I wasn't being unfaithful to myself; nothing else mattered. But when I caressed Diana Soren's hand with the tips of my fingers, I had the sensation that the infidelity, if there was any, had to be double.

After all, Diana was married to Ivan Gravet, a very popular, prizewinning French writer who'd written two beautiful books about his youth, the first about his escape from Eastern Europe, the second about when he'd fought in the war. His latest novels seemed written for the movies and were produced in Hollywood, but in everything he wrote there was always both intelligence and a growing disenchantment. I could imagine him capable of a final joke, excessive but devoid of illusion. He was a fellow writer. Could I betray him? He himself, if he was like me, would say books are more valuable than women ... I began to desire Diana.

Encounters between a man and a woman take place on two levels. One is external—filmable, if you like—the level of gesture, attitude, eyes, movement. More interesting is the internal level, where sensations, questions, doubts, games you play with yourself, fantasies begin to materialize and crowd in. She herself: what could she be thinking, what's she like, what can she be thinking about me? Facing the charm of that blond head, sculpted like a helmet for medieval warfare or for the street fighting of the 1960s (fading into the distance that night, suddenly as far off as the Hundred Years' War), I imagined an overwhelming carnal invitation, Diana Soren's head saying to me, Imagine my body, I command you. Each detail of my head, my face, has its equivalent in my body. Search my body for the smile of my visible mouth, search my body for the dimples in my cheeks, search my body for the breathing of my turned-up little nose, search for the tactile

31

and excitable counterpart of my eyes, search for the twin companion of my smooth blond hair, freshly washed, short, sometimes combed, otherwise free as the wind, but near, ever so near to its most intimate, invisible, insecure model: my flesh.

That was one level of my incipient desire as we chatted amiably on the sofa in Eduardo Terrazas's house. I must not reveal it: another clause in the constitution of encounters orders us never to give a woman the ammunition she can store up to fire at you when she needs to attack you (which, one day, she will). It's something inherent in women: to store away our sins and dump them on us when they need to and when we least expect it. Self-defense? No. Women are great at the art of making us feel guilty. To disguise my own immediate desire, I resorted to the anti-aphrodisiac idea of woman as producer of guilt, woman as the true Federal Reserve or Fort Knox of Guilt. They stockpile guilt to avoid inflation and then release those ingots of reproach little by little, distilled, wounding, poisoned, ultimately victorious, because we men, marvelous paradigms of generosity, would never do that . . . I thought about the unfaithfulness that in my case had already been consummated even if nothing had taken place with Diana Soren. I thought about Luisa, alone back in the San Angel house, and the unfaithfulness she might perpetrate if I went ahead with my own that night. More than ever, I decided it must be a double infidelity, shared, that would link us and excite us . . .

Luisa and Ivan—our absent witnesses—suspended like two exterminating angels over our bodies but respecting our unfaithful integrity because, after all, they loved us, remembered us with pleasure, and never lost the hope of being with us. And did we have the hope of being with them?

We talked of other places, other friends scattered around the world, and we felt that what was beginning to link us was not only that cosmopolitan, footloose fraternity but also the price of membership in it. To be from everywhere, we said, was to be from nowhere . . . Where would she feel comfortable? In Paris, in Mallorca, she said. Los Angeles? She laughed. A place that looked horrible externally, physically, and was horrible inside as well, hopeless.

"There's a word in English that's perfect for Hollywood: *smug*. How do you say that in Spanish?"

"*Pagado de sí, satisfecho de sí mismo*: both mean smug."

"I like them both." She laughed. "You know—the presumption of being universal. The navel of the world. Whatever happens there is the most important thing in the universe. The rest of us are just hicks . . ."

"*Payos* in Spanish."

"Only Hollywood is international, cosmopolitan. And boy, when you prove to them they aren't cosmopolitan, they hate your guts. They make you pay for it. They hate your guts."

"How can you tell? They're all hiding behind those tan masks they call faces."

"So are you!" She laughed, opening her eyes wide in mock astonishment, staring at the tan I'd brought back from Puerto Vallarta. She made me remember I'd gotten a good burn down there, in more ways than one.

That smile enchanted me. She could repeat it, I told myself, as many times as she wanted, for centuries, without ever boring me. Diana Soren's smile and musical laugh, so lighthearted, so alive that New Year's Eve in Mexico. How could I not adore her right then and there? I bit my lip. I was adoring an image I'd seen, pursued, and pitied for fifteen years . . . My vanity spurred me on. I wanted to go to bed with a woman desired by thousands of men. I wanted to feel her under me and feel the green breath of a hundred thousand green men on the back of my neck, all wanting to be me, to be where I was. I stopped short. How would she ever be able to share that pride and that vanity with me?

All that night, I underestimated the feminine capacity for conquest, the Don Juanism of the opposite sex. We don't like to admire in a woman the perseverance or luck we admire in ourselves. Our vanity (or our blindness) is huge. Or, perhaps, they reveal a secret modesty that can be a person's greatest attraction, his secret, irresistible weakness appealing unconsciously to the embrace of the mother-lover-protector who discovers the enigma of our vulnerability, which we've so carefully disguised, hidden, repressed . . .

Diana returned repeatedly to the theme of home and exile. She asked me if I knew James Baldwin, the black writer exiled in France. No. He was a good friend of my pal Bill Styron, but I didn't know him. I'd only read his books.

"He says something." Diana's eyes focused on the colonial chandelier from which the sagging New Year's Eve balloons hung like sad, dead planets. "A black and a white, because they're both Americans, know more about themselves and about each other than any European knows about any American, black or white."

"Do you think you can go home again?" I asked.

She shook her head again and again, drawing up her legs and bringing them together so she could rest her forehead on her knees.

"No. You can't."

"Do you ever go back to your hometown?"

"Sure. That's why I know you can't go back."

"I don't understand."

"It's a farce. I have to pretend I love them."

She lifted her head. She looked at my inquisitive face and quickly said, as if to rid herself of it for good, "My parents. My friends from school. My boyfriends. I hate their guts."

"Because they stayed there, in the rut?"

"Yes. But also because they saved themselves there. They didn't have to act out roles the way I do. Maybe I hate them because I'm jealous of them."

"You're an actress. What's so strange . . ."

"Iowa, Iowa." She laughed with a touch of desperation. "I don't know if we Americans should all go into exile as Baldwin and I did or stay at home as my parents and boyfriends did. Maybe our mistake, the mistake of the United States, is to go out into the world. We never understand anything going on outside the front door. We're a bunch of *payos*, as you say, hicks. Hollywood! Just imagine: if you don't know the most recent gossip, who's sleeping with who, what everyone's salary is, they think you're a moron, an illiterate. All their jokes are about provincial, local subjects. Inside jokes, you know? They don't understand someone like me, who never gives them the pleasure of repeating gossip or even of telling them about my love life."

"Baldwin also says that Europe has what you Americans need—a sense of tragedy, of limits. On the other hand, you do have what the Europeans lack—a sense of life's unlimited possibilities . . . An energy that . . ."

"I like it. I like that. What you just said."

Diana's burning hand in mine when the party ended and only she, Terrazas, and I were left. Diana invited us to have a nightcap in her hotel suite, and Eduardo said he'd drop us off while he went to pick up a girlfriend at Anderson's on Paseo de la Reforma. He'd catch up with us at the Hilton, which wasn't far away.

He never showed up. Diana and I had fun writing joint telegrams to all our friends in Paris. We went on talking about Hollywood (she), Mexico (I), drinking champagne and beginning to play with each other, while I swore that I'd never love her, that love's space was too vast for me to sacrifice it to love, that on that very night I could have substituted other women for her, lots of other women, that loving her, nevertheless, was an exciting temptation, and that I never wanted to wonder later if I could deprive myself of her . . . That night, yes, I could have left her, invented any damn pretext and walked out of that suite, which looked like an M-G-M set in a hotel destined to collapse in the next earthquake.

While she undressed, I looked out the bedroom window at the statue of the Aztec king Cuauhtémoc holding his spear on high, standing guard over the pleasures of the city he'd lost.

# VI

That long, marvelous first day of January 1970 in the Hilton suite, we didn't bother to get dressed, just wrapped ourselves in towels whenever the room-service people came. We discovered a thousand details that linked us: we were both born in November—Scorpios can sense each other. At first, I called her a *gamine*, but she didn't like it, so I stopped. But we both liked another French word, *désolé*, desolate, I'm so sorry, and we said it all the time, *désolé* about this, *désolé* about that, especially when we asked each other for physical love: we pronounced ourselves *désolés*, I'm so sorry, but I would like to kiss you, I'm sorrier, but you could come closer . . . desolate, the two of us.

Close to her. Whenever I was, everything else faded into the background, vanished like the night itself as the first light of the new year broke over the intersection of Reforma and Insurgentes. My lovely, sinister city, center of all beauty and all horror, México, D.F. All too frequently, the only thing that would bring people together in my city was solitude, a craving for company, a group, the need to belong. Even sex in Mexico City, once you're above a certain income bracket (everything here is determined by brutal class differences), is like going down a slide, riding a toboggan of pleasures—uncertain, partial, immediate—that are never postponed and end only with death. Then, when we die, we realize we were always dead.

Not Diana. She infuriated Beverly Hills gossips because they never knew whom she was sleeping with—in a city where every woman announced such things publicly. What she was doing now, it was clear to me, was an act of total commitment, one she desired, not an accident but at the same time, I sensed without knowing why, dangerous. I told myself, as afternoon came on and I remembered the pleasure of making love with Diana, that we had no illusions about each other, neither of us. Our relationship was a passing one. She was here to make a film, I was the lucky boy at a New Year's Eve party. Transitory but not gratuitous, not a *pis aller*, not a *better-than-nothing* or, as we say expressively in Mexico, a *peoresnada*—"worse would be nothing." Worse would be nothing, no one, Mr. Nothing, wiseguy. Mexicans and Spaniards delight in denying or diminishing other people's existence. Gringos, Anglo-Saxons in general, are better than we are, at least in this respect. They have more concern for their fellowman, more than we do. Maybe that's why they're better philanthropists. Our cruel aristocratic spirit, the hidalgo dressed in black, hand on chest, is more aesthetic but more sterile.

I was intrigued with the idea of discovering precisely what Diana's internal quality of cruelty, of destruction was, even if—as we all knew—she fervently supported, and was committed to, liberal, noble, sympathetic causes. Her name was on every petition against racism, in favor of civil rights, against the OAS and the fascist generals in Algeria, in favor of animal rights . . . She even had a sweatshirt imprinted with the image of the supreme 1960s icon, Che Guevara, transformed after his brutal death in 1967 into Chic Guevara, savior of all the good consciences of so-called radical chic in Europe and North America, that capacity of the West to find revolutionary paradises in the Third World and, in their lustrous waters, wash away its petit-bourgeois egoism . . . Was there any doubt about it?

Ernesto Guevara, dead, laid out like Mantegna's Christ, was our era's most beautiful cadaver. Che Guevara was the Saint Thomas More of the Second (or Millionth) European Discovery of the New World. Ever since the sixteenth century, we've been the utopia where Europe can cleanse itself of its sins of blood, avarice, and death. And Hollywood has been the U.S. Sodom that waves revolutionary flags to disguise its vices, its hypocrisy, its love of money pure and simple. Was Diana different, or was she just one more in that legion of Californian utopians, now purified, thanks to her husband, by French revolutionary sentimentalism?

I never stopped having these thoughts. But Diana's charm, her seduction, her infinite sexual capacity intoxicated me, intrigued me, obliterated my better judgment. After all, I said to myself, what could I criticize in her that I couldn't just as well criticize in myself? Hypocrite actress, my double, my sister. Diana Soren.

I had a peach taste in my mouth. Let me admit it: before that night, I knew nothing about fruit-flavored vaginal creams. During the nights that followed I would discover strawberry, pineapple, orange flavors, reminding me of the ice creams I loved to lick, when I was a boy, in a marvelous ice-cream parlor, the Salamanca, where unique Mexican fruits turned into subtle, vaporous snows, melted at the peak of their perfection when they touched our tongues and palates, yielding their essence in the instant of their evaporation. I would imagine Diana with the tastes of my childhood in her vagina—mamey, guava, sapodilla, custard apple, mango . . . She made marvelous use of this bizarre commercial product, fruit-flavored vaginal cream, which my imagination could take hold of, something it could never do with the lingerie she kept in the hotel-room dresser. I won't try to describe that. It was indescribable. A provocation, a gift, a madness. The quality of the lace and the silk, the way it intertwined, opened and closed, revealed and concealed, imitated and transformed, appeared and disappeared, contrasted wonderfully with that androgynous warrior-maiden simplicity I've already noted: Diana the fighting saint, Diana the Parisian *gamine*. I censored myself. She hated that word. *Désolé.*

What a glance, only a glance (because something kept me from touching the contents of her dresser, delighting in those textures) made me do was to see, touch, and delight in the flesh that could be hidden within such delirious objects. How incredible: a girl dressed in a T-shirt and jeans, and underneath that ordinary costume the intimacies of a goddess. Which goddess?

She herself gave me a clue the second night of our love. During the first, she had secretly guided me toward her lingerie by sitting on my lap and changing her voice, whispering into my ear in a little girl's voice, lift up my little skirt, you will lift up my little skirt, won't you? aren't you going to touch my panties? touch my panties, honey, pretty please with sugar on it, lift up my little skirt and take off my panties, don't be afraid, I'm only ten years old but I won't tell anyone, tell me what you're touching, darling, tell me what you feel when you lift up my little skirt and touch my little pussy and then you take off my panties.

The second night, naked, stretched out on the bed, she evoked other spaces, other lights. She was in the auditorium of her high school in Iowa. It was nightfall. Outside, it had snowed. All day, they'd been rehearsing carols for the Christmas Eve party. She and he had stayed behind to practice a bit more. It gets late, suddenly the December night falls, blue and white. There was a skylight in the auditorium. Leaning back, the two of them looking up, they saw the clouds scud by. Then there were no more clouds. There was only the moon. The moon illuminated them. She was fourteen. That was the first time she made love completely, virginally, with a man . . .

It was then I found out which goddess she was, or rather, which goddesses, because she was several. She was Artemis, Apollo's sister, virgin hunter whose arrows hasten the death of the impious, goddess of the moon. She was Cybele, patron of those orgiasts who in her honor castrated themselves by moonlight, surrounding the goddess flanked by the lions she used to dominate nature. She wore a crown of towers. Diana was Astarte, Syria's nocturnal goddess, who, with the moon under her control, moved the forces of birth, fertility, decay, and death. She was, finally and especially, Diana, her own name, a goddess whose only mirror is a lake where she and her tutelary sphere, the moon, may reflect themselves. Diana and her screen. Diana and her camera. Diana and her sacrifice, her celebrity, her arrows rising and falling in the implacable ratings of the box office.

She was Diana Soren, an American actress who came to Mexico to make a cowboy film in some spectacular mountains

41

near the city of Santiago. Filming would begin tomorrow, January 2, in set 6 of Churubusco Studios, Mexico City.

On the set, she stopped belonging to me. The hair people, the makeup people, the costume people took control of her. But Diana would trust her real makeup only to Azucena, a Catalan, her secretary, lady's maid, cook, and masseuse. That first morning on the set, marginalized, I had a great time examining the ointments Azucena used to make Diana beautiful. My mouth still tasted of peach. My Joan of Arc was lubricated with formulas that would have caused any medieval witch to be instantly burned at the stake if she had dared supply them secretly to the desperate, unsatisfied women in the villages of Brabant, Saxony, and Picardy. A concentrated anticellulite, multithinning gel to be applied daily to the stomach, hips, and buttocks until it completely penetrated her biomicrospheres; a thinning transdiffuser based on osmoactive systems of continuous diffusion; a restructuring and lipo-reducing cream to combat fatty skin; a translucent pink exfoliant foam to eliminate dead cells; an avocado and marigold unguent to soften her feet; an ox- marrow mask . . . My God! Could any of those concoctions be good for anything? Would they survive a night of love, a big bash, a good screw, a PRI political speech? Did they merely postpone what we all saw, a world of fat, wrinkled women with cellulite? Did the ointments mask death itself?

And only then, prepared by all that sorcery, both of us surrounded by the clamor of a movie set, isolated in the intimacy of her dressing room on wheels, did we surrender ourselves joyfully to Diana's demanding, inexhaustible love. Covered with balsams but asking to be used—use me, she said, use me up, I want to be used by you. Would I have the refined sense to recognize limits, so I wouldn't pass from use

42

to abuse? She kept me from finding out. I never knew a woman so demanding yet so giving at the same time, smeared with ethereal, perfumed, tasty ointments without which, Diana, I would no longer know how to live.

Love is doing nothing else. Love is forgetting spouses, parents, children, friends, enemies. Love is eliminating all calculation, all preoccupation, all balancing of pros and cons.

It began with the scene on my lap with the panties.

It culminated in the memory of the auditorium, the snow-covered ground, and the light coming through the skylight.

She screwed without stopping.

"Someday," she said, laughing, in excellent humor, "I'll be in a state of total subjectivity. I mean dead. Make love to me now."

"Or in the meantime . . ."

She invited me to go with her on location in Santiago. Two months. The studio had rented her a house. She hadn't seen it yet, but if I went with her, we would be happy.

We parted. She went on ahead. I decided to follow her, wondering if literature, sex, and a lot of enthusiasm would be enough. I left a note for Luisa, begging forgiveness.

# VII

"You're a complete nut." Diana laughed when I reached the house in Santiago. She took me by the hands and, still facing me, ran backward without tripping, light and barefoot, to her bedroom. "Azucena, bring in the gentleman's bags," she said to her lady's maid, and to me, "See? I already know the house backward and forward. I can find my way around it blindfolded. It's easy: the place may not be big, but it sure is ugly . . ."

She laughed again, and I agreed. In the taxi from the airport, I had caught a glimpse out of the corner of my eye of the cathedral in the town square: two high, elegant, airy towers with balconies at each of the three levels of the ascent, and I had asked myself why the Spaniards build for eternity while we modern Mexicans build things that last only one presidential term . . . Santiago was never a big city, just an insignificant frontier town for daring adventurers who went looking for gold and silver and found mostly iron. To get it out they had to take on a few Indians, and they were more interested in practicing their archery than in killing criollos. I looked in vain for that other stage in our urban architecture which I think elegant, the neoclassical, or for even the Paris-inspired buildings of the Porfirio Díaz era, but there was none of either to be found . . . Boring cement, broken glass along the tops of walls, the instantaneous, instantly disintegrating, a stillborn modernity, a Nescafé architecture that spread out from the town square toward the house reserved for Diana, a one-story modernist cave, indescribable: entrance through the garage; interior patio with wrought-iron furniture; a good-sized living room with indescribable furniture draped with serapes; bedrooms; and I don't know what else. I've forgotten everything: it was a house without permanence that didn't deserve being remembered by anyone.

Diana's enthusiasm inhabited it, the only lavishness or distinction the house could boast. I was amazed by her good spirits. Here we were in a literally godforsaken village, as if God, wanting to take revenge on mankind for having disillusioned Him so, sent these people to live on this dry, rocky plateau, burning by day, frozen by night, a hard, use-less crown of volcanic rock surrounded by canyons, cut off from the world as if by a huge knife, as if God Himself had not wanted anyone to come here except those condemned for their sins.

"Everyone says this is the most boring place in the world," said Diana as she set about neatly hanging my clothes in the closet. "Who knows how many Westerns have been shot here? It seems the landscape is spectacular and the local sal-aries low. An irresistible combination for Hollywood."

It was true. That very weekend, we discovered there were no restaurants although plenty of pharmacies, no foreign papers except the indispensable *Time* and *Newsweek*—though these were already a week old, their news stale. As for nightlife: there weren't even amusing attempts at inventing impossible "tropical" spots in the Mexican mountains, only bars that stank of beer and pulque, from which soldiers, priests, minors, and women were excluded by law, and one moviehouse, which specialized in Clavillazo's comedies and in fleas. Television had yet to extend its parabolic wings toward the universe, and no one on the set would waste a single minute watching a Mexican soap opera in black and white. The gringos would go into raptures of nostalgia watching ads for Yankee products. That's it.

Diana's hairdresser offered to cut my hair to save me from the boot-camp haircuts that seemed to be the fashion among Santiago men. They used an ultramodern method: put a bowl on top of the head and mercilessly cut off everything that pokes out from underneath it. The nape of every masculine neck boasted that abrupt cut, which resembled the local ravines. Betty the hairdresser, as I said, decided to spare me that horror.

"How good it is you came," she said as she wet my hair. "You saved Diana from the stuntman."

I shot her a questioning look. She picked up her scissors and asked me to keep my head still.

"I don't know if you've seen him. He's a very professional guy, good at his job. They use him a lot in Westerns because of how he rides, but especially for how he falls off a horse. He's been after Diana since the last picture we made in Oregon. But the competition there was stiff."

Betty laughed so hard she almost left me looking like van Gogh.

"Careful."

"He said he'd conquer her in Mexico. And then you turned up."

She sighed.

"Being on location is really boring. What do you expect a girl to do without a boyfriend. We'd go crazy. So we make do with what's around."

"Thanks a lot."

"No, they said you were tender, passionate, and cultured. Actually, you look good."

"I already thanked you once, Betty."

"If you go onto the set, you'll see him. He's a short guy but leathery, nicely broken in, like a saddle. Blond, with suspicious eyes . . ."

"So why don't you grab him?"

Betty laughed with pleasure, but there was more pleasure than fun in that laugh.

Betty's comments about the last location in Oregon set me to imagining things. I tried to convince myself, perversely, that the only way to love a woman is to know how other men loved her, what they said about her, and what they were like. I didn't bring this up with Diana; it was too soon. I held it back for a moment I foresaw as inevitable. On the other hand, I could tell her that if she made love today, she'd do it only with me, but if she died today, she would die for all her lovers; all of them would think about their love with her with as much right as I would.

I told her that one cold night when the freshly washed, still moist sheets kept us from falling asleep, annoying us, making us aware of the discomfort that surrounded us in this place but that we were intent on overcoming, beginning with the cold sheets: we'd warm them up. Our love was going to be invincible.

"I'm alone with you only as long as you're alive, Diana. I can't be alone with you if you die. All the ghosts of your other loves would accompany us. They'd have the right, they'd be justified—don't you think?"

"Oh, darling, the only thing that scares me is thinking that one of us, you or I, could die before the other. One of us would be left alone; that's what makes me sad . . ."

"Swear that if it happens, we're going to imagine each other as hard as we can, Diana, as hard as we can. You'll imagine me, I'll imagine you . . ."

"As hard as I can, I swear . . ."

"As hard as we can, as hard as we can . . ."

She said that the only real deathbed is the bed we sleep in alone. I'd told her that death is the greatest adultery, because then we can't keep others from possessing the one we love. Yet in life, I knew from experience, I should avoid even the slightest glint of possessiveness in my eyes. Despite our passionate words, I didn't want to lose sight of the transitory nature of our relationship. I was afraid of falling in love, of really giving my heart to Diana. Even so, no matter what I wanted, I could see the possibility. I relieved my fear the first night of our shared life in that high Mexican desert by summarizing my perverse fantasy in an almost scientific idea.

"We all form triangles," I told her. "A couple is only an incomplete triangle, a solitary angle, an abbreviated figure."

"Norman Mailer wrote that the modern couple consists of a man, a woman, and a psychiatrist."

"And in Stalin's Russia they defined Socialist Realist literature as the eternal triangle made up of two Stakhonovites and a tractor. Don't make jokes, Diana. Tell me what you think of my idea: We all form triangles. All we have to do is discover which. Which?"

"Well, you and I and your wife are already one. My husband, you, and I are another."

"Obviously. There must be something more exciting, more secret . . ."

She looked at me as if she was holding back, as if she loved my idea but at the same time rejected it for the moment . . . I felt (or tried to imagine) that she hadn't rejected it completely, that there was something exciting about the idea of each of us having a lover on the side, but there was something much more exciting in sharing the bed with a third person—man or woman, it didn't matter. Or taking turns—a woman for her and for me one night, a man for the two of us on the next . . .

We were in our romantic phase. We quickly returned to the plenitude of the couple we were, without need for supplements. And we went back further, much, much further, to an adorable sentiment she expressed.

"I'm anguished by the idea of couples who miss each other."

"I don't get you."

"Yes, couples who might have been but who never were, *les couples qui se ratent*, understand? Couples who pass like ships in the night. That really distresses me. You realize how that happens, how often?"

"All the time," I said, caressing her head resting on my chest. "It's the most normal thing."

"How happy we are, sweetheart, how lucky . . ."

"*Désolé*, but we're too normal."

"*Désolé*."

# VIII

We discovered that the pharmacy in the town square, exactly as in Flaubert's novels of provincial life, was the social center of Santiago. We amused ourselves seeing what it sold that could not be found elsewhere or what ordinary things in Europe or the United States were unavailable. The perfume section was horrible, all local products with a cheap nightclub smell. They made you want to go to church, inhale incense, and be purified. Any sign of MacLean's toothpaste, Diana's favorite? Not a chance. Bermuda Royal Lyme, my favorite aftershave? We were doomed to Forhans and Myrurgia. We quietly laughed, united in the citizenship of international consumption. Mexico! Land of high tariffs and industries protected from foreign competition!

Santiago's university students would meet at the door of the pharmacy, and one of them came over to me one morning when I went there alone to buy razor blades and glycerin suppositories for my chronic constipation. He told me that he'd read some of my books, that he recognized me and wanted to tell me that in Santiago the governor and the other authorities had not been elected democratically but had been imposed from the capital by the PRI. They didn't understand local problems, much less the problems of the students.

"They think we're all peons and that we're still in the age of Don Porfirio," he said. "They don't realize things have changed."

"Despite 1968?" I asked.

"That's the serious part. They just keep going on as if nothing happened. Our parents are peasants, workers, business people, and thanks to their labor we go to the university and learn things. We tell our parents we have more rights than they think. A peasant can organize a cooperative and tell the mill owner to grind up his mama . . ."

"Who's probably a grind herself," I said, without getting even a smile out of the student.

He went on, and I knew I could never expect humor from him. ". . . or the truck owners, who are the worst exploiters. They decide if they'll carry the harvest to market, when, and for how much, and no discounts. The crops rot. A worker has the right to form associations and doesn't have to be under the thumb of the thugs from the CTM."

"That's what you tell the people who work here?"

He said he did. "Someone's got to inform them. Someone's got to make them aware of things. Maybe you yourself, now that you're here . . ."

"I'm writing a book. Besides, I don't want to compromise my North American friends. They're working and can't get involved in politics. It would be a real pain if they did. I'm their guest. I have to respect them."

"Okay. Maybe another time."

I shook hands with him and asked him not to take offense. We could get together sometime for coffee. He smiled. His teeth were terrible. And yet he was tall, graceful, with languid eyes, and a sagging Zapata mustache—thin, like his unfinished, patchy, almost pubic beard.

"My name is Carlos Ortiz."

"Well, well, we're namesakes."

That he liked. He thanked me for saying it and even smiled.

At night, Diana and I went on building our passion. I didn't dare ask her anything about her past loves, and she didn't ask me about mine. I'd ventured two ideas: the company of death and the natural tendency of couples to form triangles. In reality, what both of us wanted at that stage was to feel ourselves unique, without precedents, one of a kind. The first nights were a matter of words and acts, acts and words, sometimes the one first, other times the other, rarely both at once, because the words of sex are unrepeatable, infantile, often filthy, with no interest or excitement except for the lovers themselves.

On the other hand, the words before or after the act always tended, during those early days in Santiago, to proclaim the joy and singularity of what was happening to us. With Diana Soren in my arms, I came to feel that I had written nothing before I met her. Love meant starting over. She fed and strengthened that idea: she actually told me that we were getting to know each other at the creation, before the past, before Iowa and the little skirt and the moon—she actually said that. Ultimately, she transmuted everything (and I thanked her for it) into a fantastic vision of joy as simultaneity. Sometimes during orgasm she would shout, "Why doesn't everything happen at the same time?" It wasn't a question; it was a desire. A fervent desire in which I joined. Welded to her flesh and her words. Yes, please, let *everything* happen at the same time . . .

We were unique. Everything began with us. Then literature butted in. I remembered Proust: "To know Gilberte again, as in the time of the creation, as if the past did not yet exist." And from there it was only a step to the Lucho Gatica bolero that sometimes floated through the window from the servants' rooms: "Don't ask me anything more, / let me imagine / that the past doesn't exist / and that we were born / at the very moment when we met . . ."

It's true she hadn't read the sentence in a novel by her husband, Ivan Gravet, where he says, more or less, that a couple exists while it can invent itself or because shit's better than solitude. A couple's problems begin when the two of them stop inventing themselves.

I preferred to think I was captured inside the body of this woman like a fetus that grows and fears, when it's thrown into the world, that it loses its nourishing mother, Diana, Artemis, Cybele, Astarte, first goddess . . .

"I love your cloudy brow," Diana would say when I thought these things.

"But you always have a clear brow."

"Ah," she exclaimed, "if one day you see me suffer, you'll pay for it."

# IX

No sooner did I move into Diana's house than I claimed, like some sixteenth-century Spanish explorer, a territory of my own. There I arranged my portable typewriter, my paper, and my books. Diana looked at me with smiling surprise.

"Won't you be coming to the set with me?"

"You know I can't. I write from eight in the morning until one—it's the way I work."

"I want to show you off on the set. I want to be seen with you."

"I'm sorry. We'll see each other every afternoon, when the day's shooting is done."

"My men always accompany me on the set," she said, accentuating the smile.

"I can't, Diana. Our whole relationship would fall apart in twenty-four hours. I love you at night. Let me write during the day. If you don't, we'll never get along. I swear."

The truth is, I was going through a creative crisis whose full dimensions I had yet to measure. My first novels had been successful because a new readership in Mexico identified itself (or, rather, *misidentified* itself) in them, saying *we are* or *we aren't* like that but, either way, giving an engaged, occasionally impassioned response to three or four of my books, which were seen as a bridge between a convulsed, dejected, rural, self-enclosed country and a new urban society that was open but perhaps too apathetic, too comfortable and thoughtless. One phantom of Mexican reality was disappearing, only so another could take its place. Which was better? What were we sacrificing in either case? "I'll always be grateful to you," said a woman who worked with me in the Foreign Office when I had published my first novel but still needed a bureaucratic salary, "for having mentioned the street where I live. I'd never seen it in print before in a novel. Thank you!"

The truth is, the social dimension of those books would have no real value for me unless it went along with a formal renovation of the novel as a literary form. The *way* I said things was as important as, or even more important than, *what* I was saying. But every writer has a primary relationship with the themes that arise from the world around him, and a much more complex relationship with the forms he invents, inherits, copies, or parodies—every novel contains those elements, feeds on those sources. The novel as a genre and impurity as an idea are sisters; the concept of the novel and the concept of originality are like a pair of mothers-in-law. I did not want to repeat the success of my first novels. Perhaps I made a mistake seeking out my new partnership exclusively in the idea of form and divorcing myself from subject matter. The fact is that one day I reached the palpable point of exhaustion between vital content and literary expression.

Living for several years in Paris, London, and Venice, I searched for the new alliance in my own vocation. I found it, just maybe and just fleetingly, in a funeral chant to the modernity that was wearing all of us out, Europeans and New World Americans alike. We were going to suffer a change of skin, like it or not. The upheavals all over the world in the 1960s did not help me; they only made it obvious that youth was elsewhere, not in a Mexican author who in the crucial year 1968 had turned forty.

But that was also the year of the massacre in the Plaza of the Three Cultures in Mexico City and of the Tlatelolco killings. The unpunished murder of hundreds of young students by the armed forces and government agents brought all Mexicans together, despite our biological or generational differences. It united us, I mean, in terms not only of political parties but of grief. At the same time, it divided us according to whether we supported or opposed the government's behavior. The writer José Revueltas went to jail because of his participation in the movement for reform. At a Freedom of the Press Day dinner, Martín Luis Guzmán, the novelist of the Mexican Revolution, praised President Gustavo Díaz Ordaz, who was responsible for the slaughter. Octavio Paz resigned his ambassadorship in India. The poet Salvador Novo intoned an aria of thankfulness to Díaz Ordaz and our national institutions. In Paris, I circulated petitions demanding amnesty for Revueltas and condemnations of the violence with which the government, lacking political answers, had so bloodily responded to the students' challenge.

The students were no more or less than the children of the Mexican Revolution that I had explored in my first books. They were the youth educated by the revolution, which taught them to believe in democracy, justice, and liberty. Now they were asking only for that, and the government, which had supposedly emanated from the revolution, answered them with death. The official argument until that moment had been: We're going to pacify and stabilize a country ravaged by twenty years of armed conflict and a century of anarchy and dictatorship. We're going to provide education, communication, health, and economic prosperity. For your part, you citizens are going to allow us, in order to attain all that, to postpone democracy. Progress today, democracy tomorrow. We promise. That was the pact.

The kids of 1968 asked for democracy today, and that demand cost them their lives, but it gave life back to Mexico.

I expected the new writers to translate all this into literature, but I did not exempt myself from a hard look: I accused myself of a complicity and blindness that kept me from participating in a better way, more directly, in that parting of the waters in modern Mexican life that was 1968. My recurring nightmare was a hospital where the authorities banned the students' parents and relatives, where no one bothered to tie a tag to the naked toe of a single corpse . . .

"We're not going to have five hundred funeral processions here tomorrow," said a Mexican general. "If we allow that, the government collapses . . ."

There were no processions. There was a common grave. My wife, Luisa Guzmán, sent me tranquil but secretly anguished letters: "I was rehearsing in the Comonfort theater in the Bellas Artes complex, just opposite Tlatelolco, when I began to hear a lot of shooting. I saw the government helicopters mowing down students and ordinary people indiscriminately. It went on for more than an hour, and when I left the theater the students threw themselves at me and the other actors, shouting, 'They're killing your children!' I've never heard such screams of horror and desperation. It was the worst night in many lives. The next day, the newspapers made no mention of the helicopters and said thirty people had lost their lives. No one knows how the shooting began. The kids said some agents mixed in with the demonstrators probably fired the first shots. Then someone saw them receiving arms and orders from the soldiers. Everyone has a different version of what happened. Everyone is also more and more afraid every day, not only of the violence but of what's behind the violence, and so as not to serve secret interests they prefer to serve no one . . ."

I answered that I wanted to come home to Mexico and get more involved. I'd just visited Prague. The world was changing its skin; something had to be done.

"Mexico is not Prague," Luisa Guzmán wrote back, "as you well know. The middle class is scared and is siding with the authorities, with law and order. I've talked to taxi drivers and poor people. Their ignorance and indifference are still unshakable. They swallow all the lies they hear on television or read in the papers, and they go on believing in the red-menace bogeyman. I know, I know, in spite of all that or because of it, we have to continue fighting, and if someone gets caught in the crossfire, well, it's just bad luck. But to come and put your head in the wolf's mouth only to find out it was a trap set to catch idealists seems to me absurd, sad, and even ridiculous. Student leaders disappear mysteriously, without a trace. Others have been all but killed by torture. Your only chance to take part would be from underground. Betrayal and corruption are too deeply rooted here. Perhaps there are half a dozen young people who could actually withstand the bombardment of half a million pesos, but most would end up giving in. Pardon my pessimism—I don't want to avoid responsibility, but I do want to calm down that enthusiasm you picked up in Czechoslovakia. Not a day goes by here without someone calling you, in writing or out loud, a traitor to your country. You shouldn't come back. It's all the same to me whether you're a hero or a traitor, and I refuse to talk to anyone. I'm tired of hearing superficial judgments . . ."

I did return in February 1969. One morning, angry and tearful, Luisa Guzmán and I walked hand in hand around Tlatelolco Plaza. My literary imagination would allow me only to write a theatrical oratorio on the Conquest of Mexico, another of those savage wounds driven in the body of what we call, with no clear definitions, the state, the country, the nation . . . Mexico was always sewn together with stabs, always invented by means of survival. Elena Poniatowska and Luis González de Alba wrote the great books on the Tlatelolco tragedy, and I had to content myself with admiring them, feeling they spoke in my name.

Now this accidental meeting with the student Carlos Ortiz in the Santiago plaza awakened all those feelings in me again. Not everyone had given in, as Luisa Guzmán had predicted they would. But the one who had been hiding was me; the traitor was me. I couldn't respond with the courage I owed to the loyalty and patience of my wife. I had returned to Mexico and tried to compensate for my double burden of political horror and writing block with the plaything of love, refusing—perhaps forever—to enter further into Luisa's love, to make it exclusive, to penetrate more deeply into the life of the woman who in those moments would have enabled me to venture more deeply into politics and literature. I broke Ariadne's thread. My frivolity is unforgivable. I was to pay for my abandonment of Luisa many times, again and again, in the years left to me. I just couldn't start over with her. Perhaps I should have reconstructed our love. Was it reconstructible, or was it already a great void, a lie, a repetition? Hand in hand with her, I walked Tlatelolco Plaza. Tenderness and horror mixed in my heart: was my rejection of this ceremony of death only a pretext to affirm a capacity for abstract, general love without specific content? Was I incapable of truly loving someone? Was I able to bedazzle myself by multiplying adventures only in order to convince myself, falsely, that I really could love? Why didn't I see that the love she was offering me then, at my side, was known, maybe even routine, but certain?

Tlatelolco for me was a terrible sign—my own wound as a writer and a lover—of the separation between the vital content of things and their literary expression in my work. Now, in Santiago, I was going to sit down and prove to myself that I could climb out of my hole. Anguished, I was also happy. This mad love with Diana could be my new point of departure. If the original vein of my literature had run out, what would the new one be? Would love tell me? The answer would depend on the intensity of that tenderness. That's why I had abandoned my house, betrayed my wife, exposed myself to yet another cruel fall into disillusion. How could Diana ask me to spend the day watching her get made up and have her hair done on the set? There's nothing so tedious as making a movie. I was not going to waste my time. In my name or in hers.

"You and I share something," I told Diana one cold, boring night. "We have forever lost the moment of beginning, the glory of our debut. You can lose it in movies, in literature, and in love, you know . . ."

"You're talking to a woman who stopped existing at age twenty," replied Diana. "I was a has-been at twenty."

I told her how I'd always been fascinated by that expression, the "has-been" implying a closed, finished destiny. I was too optimistic to think that way; I believe we're incomplete, unfinished individuals. I read and reread three great lines by my favorite poet, Quevedo. (Diana's never heard of him, but her secretary, Azucena, has and asks me to repeat them. Then I translate them, the three of us at the dining-room table, surrounded by tasteless white figurines in the rented house in Santiago.)

> *Yesterday's gone. Tomorrow hasn't arrived,*
> *today's going by without stopping an instant;*
> *I am a Was, a Will Be, and an Is grown tired . . .*

Perhaps what the gringos lack, I said in a joking way, is a serious sense of death instead of a tragic sense of fame. No country gives so much value to fame as the United States. It's the culmination of the great modern fanfare, that blast of trumpets which for half a millennium has been saying that "we" is not enough, that not even "I" is enough, that we need to be known, we need renown, fame. By then, Andy Warhol had already declared we'd all be famous for fifteen minutes. I asked Diana if she really believed her fame had ended when she was twenty. She rested

61

her blond, chiseled head on my shoulder and put her hand on my heart.

"As an actress, yes . . ."

"You're wrong," I consoled her. "Should I tell you what I'm going through now as a writer? I promise you we're not so different."

"Can we begin again if we love each other a lot?"

"I think we can, Diana," I said. I was deeply moved.

Moments like that don't last. The will for passion can, and I exercised it with Diana against Diana, toward Diana, with all my strength. I was convinced that she felt the same toward me, in her way. For both of us, love was always the opportunity to start over, although, for her, living was living what had yet to be lived, while for me it was knowing again how to live what had already been lived. For better or worse, I don't want to abandon my own past to a wandering orphanhood.

For Diana, her early triumph in movies and then the mediocrity of her most recent films closed the door of her profession as actress. But that was the profession she got out of bed every morning to practice. From bed I watched her reacting to the alarm clock, drinking the coffee Azucena brought her on a nicely prepared tray (Azucena is a Spanish working woman; she likes her work; what she does makes her proud, so she does it well), slipping on a T-shirt and jeans—much like her most famous character, the maid of Orléans, who discovered the most comfortable style for a warrior woman: to dress like a man—then tying a kerchief over her head, and leaving, throwing me a dry kiss as I'd steal another hour's sleep. Later I'd wake, remembering night with Diana with intense pleasure. I'd take a shower and shave thinking about what I was going to write (the shower and the razor are my best springboards for creation: water and steel; I must really be Arab, really Castilian). I watched my lover sacrifice and discipline herself for a profession in which she didn't believe, in which she didn't see her self, in which she could not even glimpse her future, while I settled down for the rest of the day in this enigma, huge and tiny at the same time: what does Diana Soren really want if what she does is not what she wants to do?

# X

The tedium of Santiago became the most tedious theme of our conversations. It seemed we'd reached an unbreachable consensus, in which all of us—Diana and I, her secretary, and the other members of the cast—concurred that Santiago was the most boring place in the world.

Instead of the well-wishing telegrams we usually send to friends on New Year's Day, this year Diana sent two or three desolate cables. They all said the same thing, just one word: HELP!

Various circles formed. The leading man, famous as the hero of a television series, lived in a large, elegant house on the outskirts of Santiago with his girlfriend and the director, a saturnine but promising man who'd also made a name for himself in television. The melancholy hotel in the center of town was home to the cinematographer—an Englishman who explicitly worshipped at the altar of Onan—and an actor who'd been famous in the workers' theater movement of the

1930s. But the sun around which the entire production revolved was the leading man, his girlfriend, and the director.

"They're very nice, and I get along well with them," said Diana. "But the deal is that we live apart and see one another very little. They like to spend their evenings drinking beer and playing poker."

Something we would never do. But I did wonder what, aside from loving each other a great deal, we would do to pass the nights. Diana told me she'd invited the character actor of the film, an American named Lew Cooper, to live with us. "Don't worry. He's sixty and very intelligent. You'll like him."

I knew very well who he was. First, because he was the greatest actor in Clifford Odets's plays during the 1930s and in Arthur Miller's in the 1940s. Second, because he was one of the victims of Senator McCarthy's witch-hunt in the 1950s. I was disgusted by all those who'd squealed on their colleagues, condemning the victims to hunger and, sometimes, to suicide. On the other hand, all those who, like Lillian Hellman, had refused to accommodate conscience to the political fashions of the day were my heroes. Cooper strangely fell between the two categories. Some said he was a totally apolitical man and that his statements to the House Un-American Activities Committee had been innocuous: he'd named those who'd already been named or who'd come forward and declared themselves Communists. He never added an unpublished name, so to speak, to the inquisitor's list. But even if he'd actually informed on no one, the moral fact is that he did give names, or at least repeat them.

How do you judge that kind of action? Cooper went on working. Others, who refused to talk, never again set foot on a movie set. Not part of the U.S. political world but from a moral world that transcended it, I was caught between my leftist convictions and my personal ethics, which rejected facile Manichaeanism and, above all, the slightest hint of Pharisaism. Was the case difficult to judge precisely because it stood between bloodthirsty, vengeful, envious, opportunistic squealing and the weaknesses and failures to which, perhaps, all of us are susceptible? Cooper's moral ambiguity made him more interesting than blameworthy. One among so many people had to be my own double. Who could reassure me that under certain circumstances I myself wouldn't have done what he did? My entire intellectual and moral self rebelled against the idea. But my sentimental side, human, affectionate, or whatever you'd like to call it, tended to forgive Cooper, just as one day someone else would have to forgive me something. There are people who replicate our weakness because we instantly recognize ourselves in them. Cooper deserved not my censure but my compassion.

Anyway, I was curious about all the people involved in the film, but Diana lost patience with my questions. "Hollywood adores capsule biographies. They save time and, best of all, excuse us from thinking. They let us put on airs of being objective, but actually we're just swallowing gossip consommé. Marilyn Monroe: a sad, lonely little girl. Irresponsible father. Insane mother. Bounced from orphanage to orphanage. She never should have stopped being Norma Jean Baker. She couldn't stand the burden of being Marilyn Monroe—pills, alcohol, death. Rock Hudson: an extremely handsome truck driver from Texas. Used to driving the highways by night, he would pick up boys and make love to them. He's discovered. He becomes a star. He's got to hide his homosexuality. He's locked in a closet filled with spotlights and cameras. Everyone knows he's a queen. The world has to believe he's the most virile of leading men. Who disillusioned them? Death, death . . ."

She laughed and poured herself a whiskey without bothering to ask me to do it for her. "Sweetheart, don't believe my biography. Don't believe it when they say: Diana Soren. Small-town girl. The girl next door. Wins a competition for the part of Shaw's Saint Joan. Wins out of eighteen thousand contestants. From anonymity to glory in a flash. A genuine sadist directs the film. He humiliates her, tries to get great acting out of her with his cruelty, but only manages to convince her she will never be a great actress. And that's a fact. Diana Soren will take any shitty part the studios offer her so she can disguise herself, so the world will believe Diana Soren is just that: only a mediocre actress. Then Diana can dedicate herself to being what she wants to be and no one can impose limits on her . . ."

I toasted her. "What do you want to be?"

"We'll be on location for two months." Her gray (or were they blue?) eyes disappear behind a veil of amber glass. "You can tell me yourself when the time's up."

# XI

We had dinner with the leading man, the girlfriend, and the director only a few times. Diana loathed that species of utopian colony which tried to reproduce Hollywood life far from Hollywood—a sublimated version, more disdainful, obvious, relaxed, and weary of what North Americans usually look for when they leave the United States. I mean home away from home, Holiday Inns identical to one another, the same towels, the same soap in the same places, the same information, magazines, filters for mental security . . . The difference between ordinary tourists and Hollywood people is that tourists, despite being afraid, live with the word *wonderful* on their lips; the world seems fascinating to them, incredible, exotic . . . but only if they can go back to their home away from home, the Holiday Inn, the same menu, every night. Movie stars, on the other hand, have seen everything, are tired, impressed by nothing. Being on location is a necessary evil—may it pass quickly; let's kill our tedium with sex, alcohol, gossip, immortality. The combination didn't surprise me. Sex told us we were alive even if the place was dead. The alcohol replaced the exceptional (because powerful and physical) nature of sex with a vaguely dreamlike, floating state that, as the leading man said, brought everything into present time: Do you realize that? All you need is a couple of martinis for everything that ever happened to you to be happening now . . .

"What do you mean, sugar? I don't get you," said his girlfriend.

"Would you like to be happy all the time?" he asked her, putting a finger under her chin and staring straight into her eyes.

"Well, who wouldn't?"

"But you're not, right?"

"So who is?"

"But when you're drinking, you're happy . . ."

"Sure, but I pay for it the next morning . . ." She laughed like a jackass.

"That's not the point. You drink and you're not only happy."

"No?"

"No. You're combining all your moments of happiness, as if you were living them all together at the same time, here and now. See?"

"Yeah, I see. Know why I love you so much? Nobody else makes me understand things . . ."

The actor laughed gutturally and hugged his girlfriend's reddish head against his hairy chest, which overflowed out of his shirt, red as a bullfighter's cape. But she shrieked because of the chain that also glittered on the actor's chest: Ow, it's hurting me, it's scraping my eyebrows . . .

He had taxidermic eyes, and when he looked at her she

swooned, saying, I've only seen eyes like that in deer trophies hanging in country clubs . . .

Sex, alcohol, and gossip. If alcohol made us happy, it also loosened our tongues: who was sleeping with whom, for how long, why, what part did they give Lilly, who'd she steal it from, who's on the way out, who's rising like the head on beer? Immortality.

"Think Lilly's going to last?"

"Don't know. Everything's relative. Last longer than what?"

"All right, less than the faces on Mount Rushmore, of course."

"Or more than who, then?"

"Garbo lasted a long time and retired at the right moment. Anna Sten lasted a minute, and they retired her at the right moment. Lupe Vélez lasted a long time but didn't know how to retire at the right moment. Death retired Valentino when he was thirty . . ."

"Look, the important thing is not what your place is but how big it is. It's the space that counts, not the time. A short time but a lot of space—you've got it made. A small space for a long time, you're a poor jerk."

"Depends on publicity. And talent, of course."

But with the word *talent* everyone's eyes became glassy; they all looked at one another as if they weren't there or as if they were all glass, like Cervantes's character, the university graduate who wakes up imagining he's made of glass. Then it was time to think about sex again, alcohol, gossip, immortality, who's going to survive, who's going to last, let's screw, let's have a drink, let's gossip, are we going to last?

I whispered to Diana that all this reminded me of one of the most repulsive institutions in the world, the gringo cocktail party, where no one deigns to concede more than two or three minutes to anyone, not the most fascinating stranger, not even one's oldest and dearest friend. Yes, you're made of glass, they look right through you to see who the next favored person is to whom they will surrender a few minutes before offering him a frozen, disdainful face, since of course waiting his turn is the next, et cetera. All of this while balancing a drink in one hand and in the other a Vienna sausage wrapped in greasy bacon, which means one shakes hands with only two fingers and with one's mouth more puffed out than the cheeks of Dizzy Gillespie playing his trumpet.

"What was it like when you went to Hollywood?" I interrupted myself.

That night, Diana did not smell of perfumed ointments. She smelled of soap and wore overalls over a white T-shirt. Only I knew the exciting delights hidden under that simplicity.

She told me many things I already knew and others I didn't.

She was chosen for the role of Saint Joan out of eighteen thousand applicants. Stardom by elimination—everything in the U.S. is like a relay race: one after another the girls were rejected because they didn't conform to the model. This one's nose was too long or short, for others it was a neck that was too long or too short; others looked too big on screen.

"The screen makes you look bigger. Ideally you have to be small and thin, or if you are big, you should be svelte and graceful in your movements like Ava Gardner, or mysterious like Garbo, or believable like Ingrid Bergman. Other girls had the most beautiful eyes in the world, but God gave them cortisone necks. Others had bodies like Venus, but moon faces."

"You're Diana, the goddess who hunts by moonlight."

She laughed. "I heard it right from the first day on the set. A very little girl for a very big part, they whispered. A great English actor took pity on me. He told me, You're going to be a star before being an actress. What horrified me were his good intentions, his pity, not the tyrannical demands of the director. He actually thought he had a clear idea of what Shaw wanted. All he asked of me was to be at the same level as the author, to be Saint Joan, and he didn't care if I was an actress or a star or if I was too small or too big for the part. Remember what Shaw says about his saint?"

I said I did, that it was a play I liked a lot. "Shaw sees the Middle Ages as a pool filled with eccentrics and Saint Joan as one of its strangest fish. Annoying everyone. A woman dressed as a man: she irritated feudal machismo. By saying she was an emissary from God, she irritated the bishops, to whom she felt superior. She gave orders to the King of France and tried to humiliate England. She told generals to go to hell and showed she was a better strategist than they were. How could they not burn a woman like that?"

Diana hung her head. "The director told me, If she'd dealt diplomatically with all of them—the kings, the generals, the bishops, and the feudal lords—she would have lived a long time. She was a woman who couldn't give an inch. She didn't know how to compromise. She was a masochist. She wanted to suffer so she could go to heaven."

She threw her arms around my neck, deeply moved, almost sobbing: What should we do, give in, stand fast, live a long life or die young, burned at the stake, what? Tell me, love.

I tried to be good-humored because my emotions were

taking control of me as well. But nothing came out; the Holy Spirit did not visit me that night. I made a sign of discretion with my finger so everyone would understand. They stared at us, shocked. I led her out to the wooden balcony that hung over a ravine. The cold night air of the desert revived us. "If only you'd directed me." Diana presented me with her dimpled smile.

"Shaw says Joan was like Socrates and Christ. She was killed and no one lifted a finger to defend her."

"I asked to see Dreyer's film *The Passion of Joan of Arc*. They—the studio—didn't want me to. They thought it would influence me. That the comparison would devastate me. Falconetti was such an infinitely sad Joan, sweetheart—I didn't have that sadness, there was no place inside from which I could extract it . . ."

"So you decided to be Saint Joan in life."

She looked at me inquisitively. "No. I decided Joan was crazy and deserved to die in the flames."

Surprised, I pressed her to go on.

"Yes. Anyone who fights for justice is crazy. Christianity is madness; freedom, socialism, the end of racism and poverty, they're all crazy. If you defend all those crazy things, you're a witch and you'll end up in the fire . . ."

Never did she look at me with greater melancholy, as if through her nocturnal eyes, so clear, were passing Dreyer's chiaroscuro images—Falconetti with her hair shaved off and her eyes bloodshot like grapes, the white walls, the bishops' black robes, Antonin Artaud's bloodless lips promising other paradises . . .

"There's a very old philosopher from Andalusia, María Zambrano, who says the following: Revolution is an annunciation. And the vigor of the revolution may be measured by the eclipses and falls that it survives. Joan was a revolutionary. She was a Christian."

"The bad thing"—she spoke with sudden bitterness—"is that the director didn't understand that . . . The idiot thought Joan was a saint because she suffered, not because she enjoyed being intolerable for everyone."

"She had to be burned," I said in conclusion, rather thoughtlessly.

"Literally, literally. The director tied me to the stake, he ordered the fire lit, and he didn't even film the scene. He watched how the flames came closer and closer to me. He wanted to see me terrified so he could make me into his Saint Joan. He should have let me be burned up then and there, the son of a bitch. The crew saved me when the flames were touching my robe. The director was happy. I had suffered: I was a saint. He didn't let me be a rebel. We both failed."

This statement restored Diana's serenity.

"To escape the director's tyranny, I married a famous writer who could dominate the director and every studio in Hollywood."

"Did he also satisfy you?"

"Never say anything bad about Ivan."

She glared at me as if I were someone else, a man made of glass, another glass graduate.

"I admire him greatly," I said with a cordial smile.

"Never laugh when you talk about him, either."

She turned on her heel and walked back into the living room. I followed her. The actor, by now very drunk, hopelessly lost in the geography of Mexico, repeated incessantly, "I'm very cross in Vera Cruz, I'm very cross in Vera Cruz"; his girlfriend wondered if Lilly, the rising star, would last or not; and the cinematographer said he had a portable solution to all problems of sexual solitude while on distant locations: he pulled down his zipper and showed us his sex (which looked like a huge bruised pear), shouting: Long live self-love! And the actor declaimed, Very cross in Veracruz, and his girlfriend begged him, Don't be a has-been. I'd leave you. I swear I'd leave you for another man. Success is my aphrodisiac . . .

"See?" whispered Diana, as the station wagon brought us to the center of Santiago. "Hollywood is a series of capsule biographies, vitamins or poison you can buy in the drugstore."

# XII

Azucena needed no capsule biography. Everything about her seemed uncertain to me at first. Her age, of course. She was short, very thin, with almost masculine sinews, which no doubt derived from a life (maybe more than one) of hard work. The nature of this job with Diana Soren was not uncertain. Azucena was invisibly involved in everything. She packed the bags for trips, unpacked them on arrival, put everything in its proper place. She made sure the clothes were always clean and pressed. She was the one who woke Diana up, brought her breakfast, and organized meals for all of us. She made the indispensable phone calls, got the plane tickets, made hotel reservations, answered telegrams, sent presigned photos of the star (how many requests, on average, came each month?), screened telephone calls, pertinent and impertinent requests. Secretary, lady's maid, deluxe servant, accomplice, bodyguard? What to call her?

Azucena. She wasn't pretty. She had one of those Catalan

faces that seem hacked out with an ax or born out of a mountain: hard, rocky, angular. Long, thin lips, long nose whose tip trembled, her stare veiled by her eyelids and thick bags, her eyes mere slits that nevertheless revealed an intelligent gleam. Everything depended on the eyebrows and the hairdo. The arc, the thickness of the eyebrow. The form, the color of the hair. Azucena had chosen a neutral hairstyle and a mahogany shade that proclaimed her message: I'll grow old with this color and this hairdo. I'll grow old and no one will notice, until everyone thinks I was always the age I was when I died.

I could never forget that on this location, only she and I knew who Quevedo was. "Yesterday's gone. Tomorrow hasn't arrived . . ." But I was curious about the real shape of her eyebrows. The artificial shape was interrogative, not a neutral declaration like her hair but a questioning challenge, arched brows from which surprise was excluded and in which, always, only the question remained.

She was Spanish, so it was easy for us to communicate. Not only because of language but because of a quality I first intuited in her and then verified. Seeing her move—agile and sinewy, always in a skirt, blouse, and cardigan, the professional city uniform of that period, but with two Spanish legs, muscular and strong, with thick ankles—I guessed there were many generations of peasants behind Azucena's leathery figure. Above all, though, there was a tradition of work, not only honorable work but pride in work. In everything the woman did, the woman took pride. One day, she told me that her grandparents were peasants from the Lower Ebro, that they'd lived in Poblet for centuries. Her parents had gone to Barcelona and set up a small grocery store; they'd sent her to study shorthand, but times in Spain turned bad and young people had to work to support their parents and siblings. She became a waitress, was hired when the Americans began to shoot movies in Spain; she met the mistress's husband—here she was . . .

She had, as I say, that dignity in her work which we associate, however much we hate the idea, with the closed European class system. It might also be the result of the ancient medieval dignity ascribed to function, to trades. When we know, centuries before and centuries after, that we were and shall be carters, bricklayers, silversmiths, innkeepers, we lend spontaneous dignity to our place, our work. This certainty—this fatality? this pride?—contrasted with the modern cult of social mobility, the upward mobility that makes us eternally unsatisfied with the place we occupy, eternally envious of those who've reached a place superior to our own, who probably did so, of course, by usurping the place that was rightfully ours . . .

Azucena didn't talk about it, but there could be no doubt she'd passed through war and dictatorship, she'd seen prison and death, she knew about the hangman's knot, and the Guardia Civil filled her with dread. But her work went on: sow, plow, sell lettuce, or wait tables. If she didn't confer dignity on her work, no one else would. The perspective of that work was continuity, permanence. She was where she was to suit herself and no one else, and that's where I saw the contrast, when I visited the set from time to time in the afternoon to meet with Diana, the hairdresser, and the stuntman. They and the other actors, the technicians, the producers, the director were all immensely anguished, hiding their anguish behind a jolly mask.

The joke, perpetual joking, is another atrocious trait of North Americans. The wisecrack, the snappy retort, the ironic or witty answer—they're all an extensive but thin mask covering the vast territory of the United States and disguising the anguish of its inhabitants, the anguish of moving around, of not being still in a single place, of arriving at another place, doing, getting things done, making it. North Americans detest what they're doing because all of them, without exception, would like to do something else so as to be something more. The United States had no Middle Ages. That's the big difference between it and Europe, of course, but it's also the biggest difference between them and us. We Mexicans descend from the Aztecs but also from the Mediterranean—the Phoenicians, the Greeks and Romans, from the Jews and Arabs, and along with all of them, medieval Spain. To get to Mexico you must travel the route to Santiago—not the movie set in Mexico but Santiago de Compostela in Spain—as did pilgrims. Later, when my Harvard students would complain about the remote traditions I dragged out to explain contemporary Latin America, I ask them: "And for you, when does history begin?"

They always answered: "In 1776, when our nation was born."

The U.S.A., sprung like Minerva from the brow of Jupiter, armed, whole, enlightened, free, envied . . . and blessed with social mobility, always higher, to be always something more, someone more, more than the person next door. The country without limits. That was its grandeur. Also its servitude.

Azucena was the lady's maid, the invisible, worthy, serenely satisfied servant. At times it was impossible to know if she was there or not. She walked through the Santiago house like a cat. One morning, she came in with the breakfast tray to wake Diana and found us screwing—well, ostensibly we were screwing: a sumptuous sixty-nine that we could not disguise. She dropped the tray. In the huge clatter, Diana and I awkwardly disconnected ourselves. By chance, because of my position or the light, my eyes caught Azucena's. In her eyes, I saw the vertigo of her imagining herself loved.

# XIII

In very tender, very vulnerable moments that I thought I was sharing with Diana, investing her with qualities, if that's what they were, or lacks of defense, which is what they turned out to be, I invited her to give it all up, to come with me to one of those North American university positions I was offered from time to time. I'd never taught in a gringo university. What I imagined was a bucolic haven surrounded by lakes, with ivy-covered libraries—and good stationers, the supreme attraction the Anglo-Saxon world holds for me.

I feel a professional distress in Latin countries: the low quality of the paper, my work material, is a negative comparable to a painter's being deprived of paint or given brushes but no canvases. The ink bleeds through notebooks made in Mexico; Spanish paper comes right out of the ancient mercantile or accounting world Pérez Galdós describes in his novels—it's first cousin to the abacus and

81

brother to parchment—and in France a sourpuss salesgirl blocks the way to any writer curious to smell, touch, or feel the nearness of paper.

In the Anglo-Saxon world, by contrast, the paper is as smooth as silk, the selection brilliant, extensive, well-ordered. To enter a stationery store in London or New York is to penetrate a paradise of writerly fruits, pens that fly like hawks, pads that are as pliant and responsive as a loving hand, paper clips that are silver brooches, portfolios as grand as protocols, labels that are credentials, notebooks that are deuteronomies . . . For years, I would go back to Mexico loaded with satin-paper notebooks for my friend Fernando Benítez so that he could write his great books about the survival of indigenous cultures in Mexico comfortably and sensually. The ideological exclusion laws of McCarthyism kept him from entering the States—he couldn't even buy good workbooks. But that's another story. The Mexican poet José Emilio Pacheco says that the first thing he does before buying a book is to open it at random and stick his nose between its pages. That magnificent scent, comparable to aromas that might be found between a woman's breasts or legs, is multiplied a thousandfold in the stacks of the great university libraries in the United States. Now I was inviting Diana, not too seriously, I admit, and with a kind of defenseless enthusiasm, I repeat. If you want, I said, we can live together in a university, you could go out and make your films . . .

She interrupted me. "It would be better than Santiago."

I was thankful for the little notes she sent me every day from location up in the mountains while I went on writing my oratorio. The best one (which I'll keep forever):

82

"My love—If we manage somehow to survive this place, we will be invincible. What can separate us? I love you." But now she said that yes, living on an American university campus would be nice. Every year, she would go back to her hometown in Iowa to celebrate the Thanksgiving that only gringos celebrate. It reminds them of their innocence, which is what they're really celebrating. They evoke the completion of the first year spent in New England by the Puritans who founded the Massachusetts Bay Colony when they reached Plymouth Rock in 1620, fleeing from religious intolerance in England.

To amuse my friends, I refer to the Puritans as the first wetbacks in the United States. Where were their visas, their green cards? The Puritans were immigrant laborers, just like the Mexicans who cross the southern frontier of the U.S. today looking for work, finding instead, sometimes, billy clubs and bullets. Why? Because they're invading—with their language, their food, their religion, their hands, and their sex—a space reserved for white civilization. They're the savages returning. The Puritans, on the other hand, enjoy the easy conscience of the civilizer. They steal land, murder Indians, decree the separation of the sexes, impede the mixing of the races, impose an intolerance worse than what they left behind, hunt down imaginary witches, and yet are the symbols of innocence and abundance. Each November, a huge turkey stuffed with apples, nuts, and spices and dripping with rich gravy confirms the United States in the certitude of its double destiny: Innocence and Abundance.

"You go back to that every year?"

She said that was actually her best role. To pretend that she was still a simple country girl. It wasn't hard for her to act out middle-class values. They were mother's milk to her; she grew up with them. "It's the role my parents expect of me. It's not hard. I tell you, it's my best part. I should get an Oscar for how well I carry it off. I become the girl next door again. The neighbor. You're right."

Her eyes veiled over with nostalgia. "Wherever I am, the last week in November I go back home and celebrate Thanksgiving."

"How do they react? Your parents, I mean."

"They serve wine. It's the only time they do. They think that if they serve wine I'll be happy, that I won't miss Paris. They see me as a strange, sophisticated girl. I make them think I'm still the same small-town girl I always was. They serve French wines. It's their way of telling me they know I'm different and they are always the same."

"Do they believe you? Do you think they believe you?"

"Let's play Scrabble. It's not even eight."

We invented different parlor games to pass the evenings. The most durable proved to be truth or consequences. The punishment for lying was a pleasure: to give the liar a kiss. Of course, it was better to say only true things and save the kisses for bed. But even though Cooper, the old actor, was alone, he wanted neither to kiss nor to be kissed.

The question that evening was one I proposed: Why do we restrain our great passions?

What do you mean? asked the actor. If we didn't restrain them, we'd go straight back to the law of the jungle. We already knew that, he said with the disdainful snort and sneering lips that characterized all his film roles.

84

No, I explained, I'm asking you to declare personally why, in most cases, when the opportunity to live a great personal passion presents itself, we let it pass, we become stupid, sometimes blind, even though it's our best chance to involve ourselves in something that would give us a superior satisfaction, a—

"Or leave us profoundly unsatisfied," said Diana.

"That's possible, too," I said. "But let's go one at a time. Lew."

"Okay, I won't say that all great passions turn us back into animals and shatter the laws of civilization. But it does happen every once in a while, from having sex with your wife to politics. Perhaps the most secret fear is that a blind, unthinking passion might rip us away from the group we belong to, make us guilty of betrayal . . ."

It was painful for the old man to go on. I interrupted him, not realizing I was breaking my own ground rule. I wouldn't let him give himself over to his passion, because I felt he was personalizing it, identifying too much with his own experience . . .

Diana shot me a curious glance, pondering my good manners, my tendency to avoid conflict . . . "You mean sex, sexual passion?"

No, said Cooper's eyes to me. "Yes," he said, "that's it. Passion takes us away from the family. It can violate endogamy. Endogamy and exogamy. Those are the two fundamental laws of life. Life with the group or outside it. Sex within or outside. Deciding that, knowing whether our blood stays home or is out there wandering around aimlessly, that's what keeps us from following great passions. Otherwise, we dive right into the abyss of the unknown. We need rules. It doesn't matter if they're implicit. They have to be fixed, clear in our mind. You marry within the clan. Or you marry outside it. Your children will either be of our family or outsiders. You either stay near the home of your grandparents. Or you go out into the world."

"Your people have gone out into the world," I said to the two North Americans. "We Mexicans have stayed inside. We even gave you half our country because we didn't populate it in time."

"Don't worry." Diana laughed. "Pretty soon California will belong to you again. Everybody there speaks Spanish."

"No," I said. "Answer the question from the game."

"You first. Ladies last." She curled up around herself like an Angora cat. Her dimples were never so deep or so promising.

"I have to admit I'm afraid of a passion that would take away the time I need to write. I've let lots of chances for pleasure pass because I could foresee the negative consequences for my writing."

"Tell us what they are." More dimples than ever, almost wanton dimples.

"Jealousy. Doubt. Time. Going around and around. Trysts. Confusions. Misunderstandings. Lies."

"Everything that takes passion away from passion," Diana said with a comic toss of her blond head.

"There is no woman you can't conquer if you dedicate time and flattery to her. Those are more important than money or beauty. Time, time, a woman devours a man's time—that's it. Dedicate a lot of time to them."

"We didn't waste any time. We saw each other and that was that," said Diana, as if she were drinking an invisible highball. "You and I."

I went on. "I'm terrified of being left with no time to

86

write. Writing is my passion. Every writer is born with a limited amount of time. From the moment you sit down to write, you begin a battle against death. Every day, death whispers into my ear, One day less. You won't have time."

"There's something worse," said Cooper. "A friend of mine who's a scientist at UCLA told me that the day will come when they'll be able to tell when you're born, first, what you're going to die of, and second, when you're going to die. Is it worth it to live like that?"

"That's another game, Lew. We'll deal with that question tomorrow." I laughed. "We've got lots of long Santiago nights left with no movies, no TV, no decent restaurants . . ."

I looked at Diana's eyes, but my gaze, imploring, not affirming, many nights ahead of us, did not dissolve the disillusion in hers. I spoke the truth. Would I deserve a kiss that night? Would Diana kiss me just to say "Did you lie? You prefer me. You'll leave everything for me. Your mornings as a writer are a farce. You live to love me at night. I know it. I feel it. Everything you write here will be shit because your passion isn't in it. Your passion is between my sheets, not between your pages."

"We should have done it," said Diana.

Lew and I looked at her, not understanding. She understood.

"Nothing should keep us from a passion. Absolutely nothing. Get me something to drink, love."

I did, while she went on to say that life is never generous twice. There are forces that present themselves once and never again. Forces, she repeated, sleepily nodding several times, staring at the polished nails of her bare feet, her chin perched on her knees. Forces, not opportunities.

87

Forces for love, politics, artistic creation, sports, who knows what else. They come by only once. It's useless to try to recover them. They're gone, mad at us because we paid them no mind. We didn't want passion. Then passion didn't want us either.

She burst into tears, so I picked her up in my arms and carried her to bed. She was the size of a little girl.

# XIV

I put her to bed: she was soft, worn out, and crying. I was getting used to the care which she seemed to require and which it gave me immense pleasure to give her. She looked like a little girl, turned on her side, crying softly, shuddering slightly in her physical smallness, begging protection and tenderness. I wanted to give it to her. I settled her on the bed, pulled up the covers to keep out the desert cold, and caressed the head I had grown so accustomed to, the Saint Joan hair, always ready for either war or fire. Unlike other women, she never left stray hairs on the pillow. In truth, she never left a trace of any kind, as if she were pure spirit, immaterial, in her Swedish, Lutheran cleanliness, as fresh as a forest, as blue as a fjord, clinging desperately to the long hours of summer, as if the winter without light were the dark mirror of death.

I saw and felt all this as I tucked her in that night while she wept and thought (I imagined) about lost opportunities for passion, the moments that passed, that called us, that we disregard, and that went away forever. It's useless to try to recover them. They're gone forever. They never turned into habit.

But, I told myself as I caressed her head and she sank into invisible dreams, everything we accept turns into habit, even passion. I smiled, caressing her blond head of very short hair; the role of Saint Joan had become a habit for Diana. She would always be a petite woman, the sparrow, the *pucelle*, the virgin, the Maid of Orléans, the battling saint, small, blond, hair cut in military style so that no one would doubt her warrior's will, so her helmet would fit properly: her hair cut very short so there would be less to burn in the bonfire. I told her silently that God would give her a halo. A head of long hair burning in the night, dragged across the night, would be seen as the trail of the devil.

Saint Joan . . . Even sainthood becomes habit, as do passion, death, love, everything. In the few weeks we'd spent together in Santiago, this bedroom had become a familiar, habitual place. We knew where to find everything. My clothes here. Hers there. The little bathroom divided equitably— which meant eighty percent for her, since she traveled with a luxurious and disconcerting variety of creams, pencils, nail polish, unguents, lotions, perfumes, lacquers . . . All I needed was space for my razor, shaving cream, my comb, and my toothbrush. I complained about the Colgate toothpaste I had to buy in Mexico, where high tariffs left us without much of a selection.

"That's a problem? What brand do you like?" Diana asked.

Half seriously, half jokingly I told her I liked Capitano, a toothpaste I used in Venice that reminded me of toothpaste my grandmother made at home in Jalapa. My grandmother distrusted products made who knows where, who knows by whom that you were going to end up putting in your mouth. She tried to do everything at home—cooking, carpentry, sewing . . . Capitano toothpaste also reminded me of my grandmother because it was pink inside and white outside. On the tube was a picture of an illustrious turn-of-the-century gentleman with a huge mustache, presumably the Capitano himself, guaranteeing the product's tradition and dependability. My grandfather, I told myself, must have looked like this nineteenth-century Capitano. My granny would have fallen in love with a man like that, with his mustache, his high, stiff collar, and his huge cravat.

"Capitano toothpaste." I laughed.

Three days later, Diana handed me a package with ten tubes of the famous toothpaste. She'd had them sent from Italy. Just like that, by snapping her fingers, from Rome to Los Angeles to Mexico City, to the provincial city of Santiago. In three days, my lover satisfied a disproportionate, sudden whim. At the same time, something that seemed to me a mere *boutade* on my part, not even a passion, took up its habitual place in our bathroom. I no longer had to *desire* my Italian toothpaste. Here it was, as if Saint Apollonia, patron saint of dentists and toothaches, had sent it down to me from heaven.

I looked at the sleeping Diana. She lived in the world of instantaneous gratification. I knew that world existed. The young people of Paris, in May 1968, had rebelled against what they vaguely called the tyranny of consumption, a society that exchanged being for seeming and took acquisition as a proof of existence. A Mexican, no matter how much he travels the world, is always anchored in a society of need; we return to the need that surrounds us on all sides in Mexico, and if we have even the slightest spark of conscience, it's hard for us to imagine a world where you can get everything you might want immediately, even pink toothpaste. I've always told myself that the vigor of Latin American art derives from the enormous risk of throwing yourself into the abyss of need, hoping to land on your feet on the other side, the side of satisfaction. It's very hard for us—if not for us personally, then in the name of all those around us.

Toothpaste from Italy in three days. A habit, no longer a desire, not even a caprice. I shook my head, as if either to exit or to enter Diana's dreams. Everything turns into habit. Diana sleeps on the right side of the bed, near the telephone and the photo of her child. I sleep on the left side, next to a couple of books, a notebook, and two ballpoint pens. But tonight, as I get into bed, reaching out to pick up a book, I raise my eyes and find those of Clint Eastwood. I drop the book in shock. Habit was broken. Diana had put a photograph of Clint Eastwood on my side of the bed, a photograph dedicated, with love, to Diana.

Those unmistakable laconic eyes, blue and icy, as intense as a bullet. His slow, spare way of speaking, as if parsimony in dialogue were a lubricant for the speed of the shot. A thin unlit cigar between tightly shut lips. It was the photo of a warrior who'd been at Troy, an Achilles of leather and stone, now transplanted far from Homer's wine-dark sea to an epic without water, coastlines, or sails, an epic of thirst, the desert, and an absence of poets to sing the deeds of the hero. That was his sadness: no one sang of him. Clint Eastwood. From under sandy eyebrows, a bitter hero stared at me between blond eyelashes. The established habit had been broken. I should have foreseen it. I always should have known that no habit would last very long around Diana. Her tears that night were only the memory of the times she should have cried and didn't.

I wanted to ask her about it someday: "Listen, do you only cry in the name of the times you didn't when you should have?"

Clint Eastwood's eyes kept me from waking her up right then and there to ask her the question whose answer I already knew. She was crying today because she didn't cry when she should have before. She had just made a movie in Oregon with Clint Eastwood. It was a long shoot. Lasted months. They were lovers. But it wasn't my place to ask anything, find out anything. It wasn't hers either. That was really an un- written law, a tacit agreement between lovers. Modern lovers, which is to say liberated ones. Not to go around investigating what happened before, with whom, when, for how long. The civilized rule was not to ask. If she wanted to tell me something, fine. I wasn't going to show curiosity, jealousy, even good humor. I was going to maintain an absolute seren- ity staring day and night at the eyes of the warrior of the West as if he'd been the Sacred Heart of Jesus, placed next to me on a night table to bless and protect us.

I wasn't going to give her the satisfaction of asking about anything. If she wanted to say something about Clint East- wood and his picture, which had suddenly appeared like a votive offering of gratitude by the headboard of our erotic bed, it was her problem. Passion and jealousy were telling me, Raise the roof, make a scene, tell this gringo whore to go to hell. My intelligence told me, Don't give her the satisfaction. She'd be delighted. Then what? Then she'd get mad at me and break up with me, I'd leave, and then? Then everything.

That was the problem: that real passion, what I was feeling for her then, kept me from doing anything to endanger my being next to her, that's all. I wasn't fooling myself. There was plenty of indignity, of an almost bitchy kind, in that. She was sticking the photo of her previous flame right down my throat and I was putting up with it. I was putting up with it because I didn't want to break up with her. I didn't want anything to break the charm of our love. But she did. That photo was a provocation. Or was it her way of telling me that both of us would have other loves after ours? I didn't want to anticipate a breakup in all that. I couldn't admit it. It would negate the intensity of my own passion, which was to be with her, screw with her, always, always . . .

Between jealousy and separation lay the road of serenity, sophistication, the civilized reaction. Pay no attention. Take it all *sans façon*. Did she want to hang photos of Clint Eastwood all over the house? Fine. I would see her as a kind of provocative sixteen-year-old, a tease, alienated, whose measles would be cured by my patient, civilized maturity. I was ten years older. Did Diana want to stick her tongue out at me? I would suck it.

But the fact is, I didn't sleep well. I wasn't convinced by my own explanation. It was all too simple. There had to be something more, and that morning, when she woke up at five and rolled over, giving and offering her daily love, my answer was almost mechanical, and afterward, getting out of bed wrapped in a towel, as if the staring eyes of Clint Eastwood and your humble servant were, taken together, a bit too much, she said this to me: "Mister, you've had two weeks of pleasure. When are you planning to give me some?"

# XV

It goes without saying that I didn't write a single line that morning. How was I going to take up the love of Hernán Cortés and La Malinche when my own had become so mysteriously complicated? What did a rough soldier from Extremadura and a captive princess, from Tabasco no less, give each other, what could they give each other? Something more than a political alliance mediated by sex? Something more than the verbal, carnal union of two languages—two tongues? By the same token, Diana went off to film a ridiculous Western in the Sierra Madre, and there I was, pondering the pleasure that apparently I hadn't given her, taking it only for myself.

For a moment, I almost convinced myself that I was like all other men, especially Latin American men, who go after their own immediate satisfaction and don't give a shit about the woman's. I was my own best lawyer: I quickly convinced myself that this didn't apply in my case. I'd showered Diana

Soren with warmth and attention; neither my patience nor my passion was in doubt. She was as voracious as I was desirous of satisfying her. If the masculine pleasure to which she referred that morning was the simple, direct pleasure of mounting her and coming, I never did it without all the preambles, the foreplay, that sexual urbanity requires in order to satisfy the woman and bring her to the point just before the culmination that leads, with luck, to shared orgasm, profound lovemaking, composed equally of flesh and spirit: coming together, soaring to heaven . . .

Did I fail in some other area? I reviewed them all. I asked her for a blowjob when I sensed she wanted to give me one, when taking her by the nape of the neck and bringing her close to my erect penis as if she were a docile slave was the pleasure we both wanted. But I also understood when what Diana wanted was slow, dazzling cunnilingus in which my tongue explored her invisible sex, when I was ashamed of the brutal obstruction of my mere masculine form, awkward, as obvious as a hose abandoned in a garden of blond grass. In her, in Diana, sex was a hidden luxury, behind the hair, between the folds that my tongue explored until it reached the tiny, nervous, quivering, dithering thrill of pure quicksilver clitoris.

There was no dearth of sixty-nines, and she possessed the infinite wisdom of true lovers who know where the roots of a man's sex are, the knot of nerves between his legs, equidistant between testicles and anus, where all virile tremors meet when a woman's hand caresses us there, threatening, promising, insinuating one of the two paths, the heterosexual at the testicles or the homosexual at the asshole. That hand holds us suspended between our open or secret inclinations, our amorous potentialities with the opposite or the same sex.

A true lover knows how to give us the two pleasures and give them, besides, as a promise, that is, with the maximum intensity of what is only desired, of what is incomplete. Total love is always androgynous.

Didn't she herself want me to sodomize her? I did it two ways, turning her over on her stomach to enter her vagina from the rear, or lubricating her anus to enter, to tear open, her most intimate bud. I covered her with oils, and one night I showered her with champagne, both of us spraying each other in a torrent of laughter; I've already spoken of her splendid vaginal aromas of ripe fruits; I sprayed my cologne in her armpits and between her legs; she hid her own perfume behind my ear, so it would stay there, she said, forever; I tricked her out like a domestic Venus, not in sea foam but in the foam of my shaving cream (Noxema), and one boring Sunday afternoon I shaved her armpits and her pubis, keeping everything in a leftover marmalade jar until it either flowered or rotted horribly, whichever.

I finally laughed out loud at all that nonsense, remembering in the end (I believed at the time) the marvelous words of Ben Jonson's lascivious millionaire Volpone, who speaks of desiring "women and men of every sex and age . . ."

Was that what was missing: sharing sex with others? Was that the pleasure Diana was talking about? What did she want? A ménage à trois? With whom? The stuntman I'd neutralized? But then why make him our third? She'd end up alone with him; I wasn't going to forgo that turn of the screw—I'd leave her alone with the man I was instrumental in getting rid of, she'd be alone with him and without the ménage à trois . . . The *partouze*, the French orgy, didn't seem terribly interesting to me or, for that matter, practicable with an old actor, a hairdresser who chewed gum, an austere Spanish lady's maid, a short, obese, bearded director, and a cameraman who proclaimed his devotion to the cult of Onan as a saving and certain pleasure during long location shoots.

With animals?

Fetishism?

The mirror. Perhaps we hadn't played with mirrors enough.

I couldn't develop that fantasy because when I looked in the mirror on one of the closet doors I saw the eyes of the Metaphysical Cowboy Clint Eastwood, and right then and there I figured it all out. I knew what Diana wanted.

Naked in bed that night I could sense her frigidity and asked her if she wanted to make love.

"Wouldn't it be better if you asked me if I like making love with you?" she said, curling up between the sheets.

"Okay. I'm asking you."

"What?"

"Do you like making love with me?"

"Jerk," she said with her most dazzling, most dimpled smile.

"I'd like to make love to you in the name of all the men who've made love with you," I told her, thrusting my mouth next to her ear.

"Don't say that." She trembled slightly.

I grasped her around the waist. "I don't know if I should say it."

"We're free. We don't hold anything back, you and I."

"There's something I like about you. You always pretend we're alone when we screw."

"Aren't we?"

"No. When we go to bed I see a horde of men pass over

your skin, from your first lover up to the ones who aren't here but who are still on the active list . . ."

I glanced at the photo of the star of A *Fistful of Dollars* and felt a chill.

"Go on, go on."

I no longer knew what I was doing with my hands. I only knew my words.

"Can there be sex between only two people?"

"No, no."

"Do you like to know that when I'm screwing you I think about all the men who've enjoyed you?"

"You have a nerve, telling me that."

"Didn't you know that, Diana? Don't you like it, too?"

"Don't say that to me, please."

"Do I disillusion you when I say that?"

"No," she almost shouted. "No, I like it . . ."

"To think that along with me all the men who've ever screwed you in your life are with me?"

"I like it, I like it . . ."

"I thought you weren't going to like it."

"Don't say anything. Feel what I'm feeling . . ."

"Why don't we dare to feel that pleasure if we like it so much?"

"Which pleasure? What are you saying?"

"This pleasure. The one I give to you thinking I'm someone else, the one you feel imagining that I, too, am someone else— admit it . . ."

"Yes, I like it, it drives me crazy, don't stop . . ."

"I wish that all of them were here, seeing us screw, you and I . . ."

"So do I, don't stop, go on . . ."

"Don't come yet . . ."

"But you're giving me lots of dicks today . . ."

"Wait, Diana, they're all watching us, from that mirror, they're watching us and they're jealous . . ."

"Tell me you like it, too, that they're looking at us . . ."

"I like that you pretend we do it alone. I like to know you like it . . ."

"I like it I like it I like it . . ."

When we finished, she turned toward me, half closed her gray (blue?) eyes that were like a forgotten mist, and said, "You have no imagination."

# XVI

Reasonably or not, I've lived to write. Literature, almost since I was a child, has been the filter of experience for me, from fear of being punished by my father to my most recent night of love. Sex, politics, soul—it all passes through my literary experience. The expectations of the book refine and strengthen the facts of lived life. Perhaps nothing of this is true, or perhaps in reality it's the other way around: it's literary imagination that determines, provokes the "real" situations in my life.

But if that's the way it is, I'm not aware of it. Yes, I would like to be aware that for me reality is not a simple fact or that it's defined by only one of its dimensions. There are people for whom reality is only the objective, concrete world—the chair is the chair, the mountain has always been there, the cloud passes over but obeys the laws of physics—all that is real. For other people, the only reality is internal, subjective reality. The mind is a vast unfurnished room that slowly but surely fills us up as we live with the furniture of perceptions. The objective world exists, but it has no meaning unless it passes through the sieve of my mind. Subjectivity gives reality to a world of mute, inanimate objects.

But there is a third dimension, which is where my individuality comes into contact with others, with my society, my culture. That is, something exists that is neither paradox nor impossibility, something called collective individuality. Within it, I feel myself to be most complete, in greatest consonance with the world. It's in that shared individuality where I find family, women and sex, friends . . . So reality for me is a three-pointed star: matter, psyche, and culture. Material reality, subjective reality, and the reality of the contact between my ego and the world. I don't like sacrificing any of them. Only when the three are present can I say I'm happy.

Our evening parlor games continued and one of them was Scrabble. Now, the alphabetic combinations change according to which language you play in: Spanish abounds in vowels, while English is rich in consonants. The English *w*, the *sh*, the double *tt*, *mm*, or *ss* make for inconceivable conjunctions in Spanish. On the other hand, we do have that clitoris of language, the *ñ*, which drives foreigners insane because they think of it as a Hispanic, medieval extravagance comparable to the Holy Inquisition, when it's actually a futurist letter that embraces and suppresses the laborious *gn* of French, the *nh* of Portuguese, and the unpronounceable English *ny*.

The three of us—Diana, Lew, and I—played like a bored, well-established family, using an English alphabet. While I know English well, it isn't mine nor I its. I've never dreamed in English. I speak it, but I'm mentally translating very fast from Spanish. It's easy to see because my English abounds in Spanish cognates, in locutions derived from Latin or Arabic rather than Saxon or German. My error that night came when I had before my eyes the word *wheel*, perfectly formed, and with six spaces after it that I could fill in to pick up some great points. All that I could think of was *wheelbarrow*, because sometimes I'd hum a pretty Irish song about "Sweet Molly Malone," who "wheeled her wheelbarrow through streets long and narrow," but though *barrow* was six letters, I didn't have the right ones. I had to pass, and Lew filled the space I coveted with his six letters, *wright*—the old Saxon word *wheelwright*. I said I didn't know that word. Diana gave me a mocking look. Then she brusquely turned my letters around and showed that I could have filled at least five of the spaces with *chair* and gotten *wheelchair*.

"So you think you're going to teach in a university in the U.S.?" she asked, her tone unbearably sarcastic. "Be careful. The students might end up teaching you."

"Do they know everything, or do they only think they know everything?"

"They know more than you, you can be sure of that," said Diana. Lew lowered his eyes and asked if we could go on playing.

But it was Lew Cooper who suggested another game for our nights of Durango tedium. Let's imagine, he said, that we're Rip Van Winkle and we've been asleep for twenty years. When we wake up, what kind of country will we find?

"Mexico or the United States?" I asked, to make it clear there was more than one country in the world.

They stared at me as if I were a complete idiot.

Cooper immediately launched into the inevitable theme of the loss of innocence, which so obsesses the gringos. I always wondered, When were they innocent: when they were killing Indians, when they took up manifest destiny and unleashed their continental ambitions from coast to coast, when? In Mexico, we cherish the memory of the cadets who threw themselves off the walls of Chapultepec Castle rather than surrender to the invading forces of General Winfield Scott. Were they just perverse adolescents who refused to hand their banners over to invading innocence? When was the United States ever innocent? When it exploited enslaved black labor, when its citizens massacred one another during the Civil War, when it exploited the labor of children and immigrants and amassed colossal fortunes acquired, no doubt, in an innocent way? When it trampled defenseless nations like Nicaragua, Honduras, and Guatemala? When it dropped the bomb on Hiroshima? When McCarthy and his committees destroyed lives and careers through mere insinuation, suspicion, and paranoia? When it defoliated the jungles of Indochina with poison?

I laughed to myself, holding back my possible answer to the question of the Rip Van Winkle game. Yes, perhaps the U.S. was only really innocent in Vietnam, for the first and last time, thinking it could, as General Curtis LeMay, head of the U.S. Air Force, said, "bomb Vietnam back to the Stone Age." How shocking it must have been for the country that had never lost a war to be losing one to a poor Asiatic, yellow people, a people ethnically inferior in the racist mind that, flagrant or suppressed, ashamed or defiant, every gringo has nailed to his forehead like a cross.

The two Yankees went on talking, and perhaps because both were actors, I imagined that the famous innocence was only an image of self-consolation especially promoted by movies. In literature, from the beginning, from Hawthorne's tortured Puritanism, Poe's nocturnal nightmares, and James's daytime ones, there has been no innocence, just fear of the

104

dark power each human being carries within himself. The enemy self, not a whale, is the protagonist of *Moby-Dick*, for instance. That's almost a definition of good literature, the epic of the enemy self . . .

I don't know if Tom Sawyer and Huck Finn are true innocents or if it's just a fine bucolic desire for contact with family (Tom) or the river (Huck) that distracts them momentarily from the obligation to make money, subjugate inferiors, and practice arrogance as a divine right. In any case, Mark Twain wasn't innocent; he was ironic, and irony is negative, according to its modern inventor, Kierkegaard, "an abnormal development which . . . like the liver in Strasbourg geese finally kills the individual." But at the same time it is a way of reaching the truth because it limits, defines, makes finite, abrogates, and castigates whatever we think true.

In American movies, the myth of innocence is created with no irony whatsoever. My childhood eyes were filled with figures from the countryside, from small towns, who come to big cities and are exposed to the worst dangers. They fight against sex (Lillian Gish), locomotives (Buster Keaton), and skyscrapers (Harold Lloyd). How I enjoyed, when I was a kid, the sentimentally innocent movies of Frank Capra, where the valiant small-town Quixote, Mr. Deeds or Mr. Smith, defeats with his innocence the powers of corruption and falsehood.

It was a beautiful myth, consistent with the moral and humanitarian policies of Franklin Roosevelt. Since the New Deal was followed by the world war and the struggle against Fascism, which not only wasn't innocent but was diabolical, the Yankees (and we along with them) completely believed the myth of innocence. Thanks to their virtue, they saved the world twice, defeated the forces of evil, identified and annihilated the perfect villains, the Kaiser and Hitler. How many times have I heard Yankees of all classes say, "Twice we saved Europe during this century. They should be more grateful."

For Yankees, as in Henry James's "international" novels, Europe is corrupt, the United States innocent. I don't think there's any other country, especially a country so powerful, that feels innocent or brags about it. The hypocritical English, the cynical French, the haughty Germans (the blameworthy, self- flagellating Germans, so lacking in irony), the violent (or weepy) Russians—none of them thinks his nation has been innocent. As a result, the United States declares that its foreign policy is completely disinterested, almost an act of philanthropy. Since this is not and never has been true for any great power, including the United States, no one believes it, but U.S. self-deception drags everyone into confusion. Everyone knows what kind of interests are in play but no one's supposed to admit it. What is pursued, disinterestedly, is liberty, democracy, saving the others from themselves.

I imagined Diana as a girl listening to Lutheran sermons in an Iowa church. What could have gone through that childish head when a pastor said that men are all guilty, unacceptable, condemned, yet that Christ accepts them despite their unacceptability, because the death of Christ gives more than sufficient expiation for all our sins? Does a doctrine of that caliber sentence us to live so as to justify Christ's faith in us? Or does it condemn us to total irresponsibility, since our sins have all been redeemed on Golgotha?

The words of the old actor had drifted far from my own musings. His Rip Van Winkle woke up and didn't recognize the nation founded by Washington and Jefferson. Lew Cooper saw what he himself lived through with his eyes wide open. He saw the terrible puritanical need to have a visible, indubitable enemy who could be named. The U.S. sickness was a Manichaean obsession that can only conceive of the world as divided into good and evil, with no redemption possible. Cooper said that no Yankee can live in peace unless he knows whom he's fighting against. He disguises that by saying he's got to figure out who the bad guys are so he can defend the good guys. But when Rip Van Winkle wakes up, he discovers that, in defending themselves, the good guys have taken on the traits of the bad guys. McCarthy didn't hunt down the Communists he saw hiding under the bed. He hunted down and humiliated and ruined Democrats, with the same methods that Vyshinsky used in the Soviet Union to fight—of course—Communists. The victims of McCarthyism, of the House Un-American Activities Committee, of the Dies Committee, of all those new-model tribunals of the Inquisition, were Washington, Jefferson, and Lincoln, Cooper said, deeply melancholic. We're condemning ourselves. Rip Van Winkle would rather return to his hollow tree and sleep twenty more years. He knows that when he wakes up he'll find exactly the same thing.

"A country that despite everything hasn't lived up to its own ideals?" I asked my fellow players.

"Right," said Cooper. "No nation has ever lived up to its ideals. But the others are more cynical. We're idealists, didn't you know that? We're always on the side of good. Wherever we are, that's where good is. When we don't believe that, we go crazy."

"We should never leave home," Diana said very simply. I remember her at that moment, sitting on the rug with her legs crossed and her hands folded on her lap. "The title of Thomas Wolfe's novel is *You Can't Go Home Again* . . . that's the truest title in all of American literature . . . You walk out of your house, and you can never go back, no matter how much you want to . . ." she added with a tired look.

I asked her if that was her case. She shook her head.

She said that when she came back after living in France, she found a whole new generation in California, in the Midwest, and on the East Coast who wanted to give the best they had but who weren't allowed to. There was a huge difference between the ideals of the young people of the 1960s and the corruption, the immense mendacity of the government, the violence pouring out of every orifice of society . . . That night, Diana said what was on everyone's mind, but she told it from her own point of view, that of a girl from the Midwest who had gone off to Paris to sleep and then, like Rip Van Winkle, had returned to the whirlwind—the assassination of the Kennedys and Martin Luther King, Jr., the deaths of tens of thousands of boys who'd gone from small towns to the Asian jungles, the dead of Vietnam, the drugged soldiers, the useless dead, all for nothing—well, at least it wasn't white boys who were out in front but blacks and chicanos, cannon fodder— and at home a chorus of liars was saying we're containing China, saving Vietnamese democracy, keeping the dominoes from falling . . . .

Johnson, Nixon, the great voices of hypocrisy, ignorance, stupidity—how could they not cause an entire generation to lose its illusions; how could they not end up shooting students at Kent State, beating up demonstrators in Chicago, jailing Black Panthers? And for what? Diana's voice rose, and she seemed to wake from an extremely long sleep behind a silver screen that was her own way of looking at the world. Not to make fortunes, not for the sake of vulgar corruption, however rich they made a hundred contractors or a dozen large defense companies; that was okay, that I can even understand, but what drives me crazy is the way those creeps fall in love with their power, believe in their power as something that not only will last but is important. My God, the idiots think their power is important—they don't know that the only important thing is the life of the boy they sent off to die uselessly in an Asian jungle, a confused boy who, to justify his presence there, burned a village and killed all its inhabitants because if he didn't why was he there, what was the use of that automatic rifle whose manufacturing provided livings for thousands of workers and their families, a single automatic rifle that gave power to Lyndon Johnson, to Richard Nixon, to the Goddess Lie, to the Whore Power?

Diana Soren was losing it. Her voice was falling into a strange, empty abyss; she would go back to sleep for twenty more years as long as she didn't have to know what was going on in that home to which she could never return . . . America was what was going on *outside* her sleep.

She pushed the button on her tape deck and out came the voice of José Feliciano singing "Come On, Baby, Light My Fire." Cooper stood up, indignant, and turned it off. He parodied Feliciano's voice. That's what we've come to. That was today's music, savage music for idiots—come on, baby, light my fire. He mimicked it hideously and excused himself to go to bed.

109

# XVII

With my prerogative to stay at home and write all day firmly established, I paid a surprise visit to the set one morning. Diana wasn't mad at me for not warning her; she received me with a big display of cheerfulness, showed me off, introduced me to everyone, and invited me to have coffee in her trailer. It was the same one we used at Churubusco Studios in Mexico City. Now, she said, with a roguish look in her eyes, we don't have to use it the way we did then. Why not? I answered.

When we left the trailer, the makeup and hair people were waiting impatiently. The director was edgy. The cloudy day was going to clear up. He peered at the sky through a very fine and mysterious apparatus, squinting one eye and wrinkling up his entire face, as if he were expecting instructions from above so he could go on filming and saving money for a company that no doubt worked at the right hand of God, with His blessing and mandate.

The landscape of the Santiago mountains falls apart and reconstructs itself according to the whims of the light. I walked across the plain toward the mountains that were storing up all the shade of the day, swaying like trees under the tricky sky. Some kids were playing soccer on an improvised field. The spectacle was funny because the goats the children were tending didn't respect the boundaries set for the game and would periodically invade, at which point the boys would stop being rustic Pelés and go back to being shepherds.

A flock of stolid lambs, their wool as curly as a filthy wig on an English magistrate, came tumbling down toward the playing field. The boy tending them was received with whistles and insults by the players. One of them even went so far as to jump the shepherd, grab his staff out of his hand, and begin to beat him with it. I ran to stop it, separated them, called the attacker a bully, because he was taller than his victim, and the other members of both teams thugs, because they were taking their revenge on the lambs who were erasing the boundaries marked out with chalk.

"Leave him alone, you thugs. It's not his fault."

"Yes, it *is* his fault," said the tall boy. "He's conceited. Who does he think he is? Just because he was Benito Juárez."

This allusion to a hero of Mexican history seemed so outrageous to me that at first I laughed. Then I grew curious. I carefully studied the boy who'd been attacked. He couldn't be more than thirteen and looked very Indian, his cheeks like two broken clay pots, his eyes reflecting an inherited sadness, passed down from century to century. He was wearing a shirt, overalls, a straw hat, and huaraches and was even tending a flock. He really was another Benito Juárez, who until he was twelve was an illiterate shepherd who spoke no Spanish and then was president, victor over Maximilian and the French, the "Benefactor of the Americas," and a specialist in coining celebrated sayings. His impassive face is in a thousand plazas in a hundred Mexican cities. Juárez was born to be a statue. This boy was the original.

I offered him a Coke, and we walked toward the movie set.

"Why do they go after you?"

"It pissed them off that I was Juárez."

"Tell me how that happened."

He told me that a year before, an English television company was there making a picture, and they offered him the part of the boy Juárez tending his flock. All he had to do was walk past the cameras with his sheep. They gave him ten dollars. The other boys were furious, even though he spent part of his money treating them all to Cokes. The rest of the money he gave to his father. The boys never eased up. They had it in for him and shut him out. He asked the English people, "When will the movie come out. Can I see it?" They said in a year. It would certainly be announced in newspapers and in TV listings. He told that to the boys, and it only made them angrier. When do we get to see you on TV, Benito? What? They're going to make you into a movie star, Benito? What a laugh!

He asked me if I knew if the film had been released and when it would come to Santiago, so he could shut these bastards up once and for all.

No, I told him, I don't know a thing about it. I've never heard anything about that picture . . .

The boy clenched his teeth and left half of the Coke. He asked permission to return to his flock.

I went back to the set. The stuntman was being filmed in a scene in which he was breaking a wild horse. He was wearing the clothes of the male lead, who was watching him from a folding chair, drinking a Bloody Mary. The director ordered a shot to be fired to agitate the pony, and then the stuntman began to break him. His eyes sought out Diana, who was sitting next to the actor, and the director stopped the action to scold him—he had no reason to be looking at the actors, he didn't need anyone's approval. Didn't he realize that he was alone on a Mexican mountain breaking a wild horse, didn't he know by now that there's a scenic illusion that consists in denying the existence of the fourth wall of the set, the one that opens onto the audience, the city, the world, to magic? The director became very eloquent, and I could see how in his eyes the student of the arts of Stanislavsky and Lee Strasberg had been reduced (or magnified, depending on how you saw it) to this task of creating an art where art must never be detected. He was good, I said. It was a good compromise. In the hands of a Buñuel, a Ford, a Hitchcock, it was the *best* compromise: to say everything with artistry so superior and intense as to be undetectable, fusing with the clarity of technical execution. An art identical to a pair of eyes watching.

The stuntman took it as joke, laughed, and said in a loud voice: "How about the Mexican writer coming over here to break the horse. Everybody says Mexicans are great riders."

"No," I shouted back. "I don't know how to ride. But you don't know how to write a book."

He didn't understand me, or he was very thick, because for the rest of the day he spent his time on practical things: he moved trailers, tied up cables, raised machines, drove horses, tested rifles, and counted blank cartridges out loud, all as if he wanted to impress me with his mechanical ability—me, who can't drive a car or change a tire. His physical exhibitionism nevertheless comforted me. Once, when the hairdresser told me that the stuntman had been after Diana since Oregon, I had imagined him inside the trailer with her while I stayed behind in Santiago filling page after page with growing diffidence and disillusion. Now, as I watched this macho show-off, I was sure he'd never touched her. He put on too much of a show, made too much of a fuss, wasn't really sure of himself. He was no rival . . .

On the way back to Santiago, Diana leaned on my shoulder and played with my nails, exciting me. We passed the boy who'd been Juárez, and I told Diana the story.

"What did you tell him?"

"The truth. That I didn't know anything about it."

She made a guttural noise she instantly stifled, raising her hand to her mouth and abandoning my nails.

"What a terrible thing to do!"

"I don't understand."

"How could you understand? You're the man whose table is always set for him. You don't know what it is to fight, to get out of the hole . . ."

"Diana . . ."

"You should have told him you knew all about it, don't you understand? You should have told him you saw the film, that he was stupendous, that the picture is a success everywhere, and that it'll be coming to Santiago soon to shut his friends up . . ."

"But that's an illusion . . ."

"Movies are illusion!" Her eyes shouted louder than her voice.

"I refuse to give these people false hopes. It's worse that way. I swear it's worse. The fall is disastrous."

"Well, I think you've got to give a hand to the person who needs it. We all need a hand . . ."

"Charity, you mean."

"Okay, charity . . ."

"So they never stop being beggars. I hate charity, philanthropy . . ."

She moved away from me, as if I were burning her, as if she herself were freezing cold.

"Tomorrow I'm going to look for that boy first thing."

"You're going to leave him worse off than ever, I'm telling you."

"I'm going to look for the film, I'm going to bring it here, and I'm going to show it to the boy, his family, his friends . . ."

"Who will hate him more than ever. They'll be jealous of him, Diana, and there won't be any sequels. He won't make any more pictures . . ."

"You have no imagination. I'm telling you, no imagination, and no compassion whatsoever . . ."

"For you, it's all Italian toothpaste . . ."

We turned our backs on each other, staring attentively at a landscape devoid of interest, abolished, erased.

# XVIII

"You left the door open."

"You're mistaken. Look at it. It's tight shut."

"I mean the bathroom door."

"Yes. It's open. So what?"

"I asked you always to keep it closed."

"Well, it so happens that at this particular time I'm going in and out a lot."

"Why?"

"What's it to you? Because I've just come down with a case of Montezuma's revenge, because . . ."

"You're lying. You Mexicans never get that. You reserve that for us . . ."

"Diarrhea recognizes neither frontiers nor cultures. Didn't you know that?"

"How can you be so horribly vulgar?"

"Why's it such a big deal whether the bathroom door is open or closed?"

"I'm asking it as a favor."

"How delicate we are. At least you're not giving me a direct order. After all, I am living in your house."

"I never said that. All I'm asking is that you respect . . ."

"Your manias?"

"My insecurity, stupid. I'm very sensitive to things that are open or closed. I'm afraid. Help me, respect me . . ."

"So our relationship is going to depend on whether I close the bathroom door or leave it open?"

"It's such a little thing. And since you put it that way, yes, you are in my house . . ."

"And you're in my country."

"Eating shit, that's true."

"We could go back to Iowa and eat fried chicken in cellophane or dog-meat hamburgers. I'm ready when you are . . ."

"Since you don't respect my vulnerability, you can use another bathroom and let me have this one . . ."

"I can also sleep in a different bedroom."

"I'm asking you to do me the tiniest favor. Close the bathroom door. Open bathroom doors scare me, okay?"

"But it doesn't bother you to sleep with the bedroom curtains open?"

"I like that."

"Well, I don't. The sun comes blazing in early and I can't sleep."

"I'll lend you an American Airlines sleep mask."

"You get up at dawn, so you're fine. But I end up with a fucking migraine."

"You'll find all the aspirin you need at the drugstore."

"Why do you insist on sleeping with the curtains open?"

"I'm waiting."

"For whom? Dracula?"

"There are beautiful nights when the moon invades a bedroom, transforms it, and transports you to another moment in your life. Maybe that will happen again."

"Again?"

"Right. Moonlight inside a bedroom, inside an auditorium, it transforms the world—that's something you really can believe in."

"You told me not to believe in your biography."

"Just believe in the images I offer you from time to time."

"Please excuse me. I'll leave the door closed. I wouldn't want a single moonbeam to escape."

"Thank you."

"Assuming one does arrive some night."

"It will. My life depends on it."

"I think you really mean, my memory."

"Don't you remember any night you'd like to recapture?"

"Lots of them."

"No, it can't be 'lots of them.' Only one or none at all."

"I'd have to think about it."

"No. Imagine it."

"Tell me what props I'd need, O Duse."

"Don't laugh."

"Duse Medusa."

"You'd need snow."

"Here?"

"Snow all the time. Snow all four seasons of the year. I can't imagine it without snow. Snow outside. A circle. A circular theater. An auditorium. A skylight. Night. Me stretched out on the stage. The two of us alone. Him on top of me. Searching with his hand. Lifting my little skirt."

"Like this?"

"Exploring me with a marvelous tenderness no other man has ever known how to give me."

"Like this?"

"He's patient, exploring, lifting my little skirt, sliding his hand under my panties, searching in the darkness . . ."

"Like this."

"Until the moon rises and the light floods over us, the moonlight shines on my first night of love, my love . . ."

"Like this, like this . . ."

"Like this. Please, quickly."

"But there's no moon. I'm sorry."

"What?"

"There's no moon here. We'll have to wait. Or if you'd like, I could buy a paper moon and hang it over the bed."

"You have no imagination, I told you already."

"Listen, don't cry. It's no big deal."

"Almost. You almost made it. What a shame."

"Here."

"What are you doing? What is this?"

"A present. In exchange for the toothpaste."

"You killed my imagination. You don't have any right to do that."

"It's three o'clock in the morning. You've got to get up very early. Want anything else?"

"Get up and close the bathroom door, please."

"Good night."

# XIX

The Santiago authorities hosted a banquet in honor of the film crew. One of the patios of the colonial-era town hall was set up with tables and chairs and decorated with crepe and paper lanterns. The functionaries were distributed equitably: the governor with the director, the municipal president with the leading man and his girlfriend, the commander of the military zone, a general of strikingly Oriental appearance, with Diana and me.

They say the French general Maxime Weygand was the bastard son of Empress Carlota by a certain Colonel López, Maximilian's aide-de-camp. López betrayed the Emperor twice: first with the empress, and then during the Republican siege of Querétaro, when he opened the way for Juárez's troops to capture the Austrian Emperor. By then, Carlota had already gone back to Europe to beg help from Napoleon III, another traitor, and Pope Pius IX. She went mad in the Vatican, and was the first woman (officially) to spend the night in the pontifical bedrooms.

Did she go crazy or was that merely a pretext to cover up her pregnancy and delivery? She never again left the seclusion of her castle, but the royal government of Belgium supplied young cadet Weygand, born in 1867 in Brussels, with tuition at St. Cyr. He became chief of Foch's general staff during World War I and supreme commander when World War II broke out. In France, the Manchu face—high cheekbones, Mayan nose, lips as thin as a knife blade and crowned by a sparse, very fine mustache, barely a shadow—must have caused some comment. Short, small-boned, with a rather stiff bearing, his black hair shaved at the temples: I'm describing General Weygand only to describe General Agustín Cedillo, commander of the Santiago military zone. I associate him with the empire imposed on Mexico by Napoleon III because, physical parallels aside, there survived on one of the balconies of the patio, surely a Republican oversight, the arms of the empire: the eagle and serpent but with a crown above and, at the foot of the cactus, the motto EQUITY IN JUSTICE.

Sitting opposite me and next to Diana, General Cedillo, curious, looked us over out of the corner of his eye, as if he kept a direct gaze in reserve for great occasions. I imagined that those could only be challenges and death. I had no doubt whatsoever: this man would look with perfect equanimity directly at a firing squad whether giving it orders to shoot or receiving its bullets. He would take care, on the other hand, not to look directly at anyone in daily life, because in our country, among men, a direct stare is a challenge and provokes one of two reactions. The coward lowers his eyes—lower your head and step aside, as the song says. The brave man endures the stare of the other to see who will lower his eyes first. The situation moves to another plane when one brave man pronounces the ritual words "What are you looking at me for, mister?" The violence increases if the "mister" is excluded: "What are you looking at me for?" And there's no way out if a direct insult is substituted: "What are you looking at me for, stupid, asshole, son of a bitch?"

Familiar with the protocol of eyes in Mexico, I looked at General Cedillo out of the corner of my eye the same way he was looking at Diana and me. Glancing around the patio, I saw that the same look was being repeated at each table. Everyone except the innocent gringos avoided one another's eyes. The governor peered surreptitiously at the commander and likewise at the governor; the mayor tried to avoid the eyes of both of them, and I saw in a corner of the patio a group of young people just standing there, among them the boy who'd approached me in the plaza to propose we talk, the boy with the Zapata mustache and languid eyes named Carlos Ortiz, my namesake.

The commander noticed my glance and asked me, without turning his head, "Do you know the students here?"

I told him I didn't, only by accident, that one of them had read my books.

"There are no bookstores here."

"How terrible. And how shameful."

"That's what I say. Books have to be brought in from Mexico City."

"Ah, they're exotic import products," I said, flashing my friendliest smile but slipping into the humorous, mischievous vein that conversations with authority figures invariably provoke in me. "Subversive, perhaps."

122

"No. Whatever we know here, we find out by reading the newspapers."

"Then you must not know much—the local papers are very bad."

"I mean the common folk."

That old-fashioned expression made me laugh and forced me to think about the commander's social origins. His appearance, I admit, was an enigma. Class differences in Mexico are so brutal that it's easy to pigeonhole people: Indian, peasant, worker, lower middle class, etcetera. What's interesting are people who can't easily be categorized, people who not only rise socially or become refined but, in rising, bring with them another kind of refinement, secret, extremely ancient, inherited from who knows how many lost ancestors—princes perhaps or shamans, or warriors in one of the thousand archaic nations of old Mexico.

If that weren't the case, where would such people get their reserves of patience, stoicism, dignity, and discretion, which contrast so strikingly with my country's noisy, vain, ostentatious, and cruel plutocracies? In reality, Mexico's two classes are composed, one, of people who allow themselves to be seduced by Western models that are alien, lacking as they do a culture of death and the sacred, and who become the vulgar, stupid middle class and, two, a group that preserves the Spanish and Indian heritage of aristocratic reserve. There's nothing more pathetic in Mexico than the vulgar middle-class joker, situated between the Indian aristocracy and the Western bourgeoisie, who says hello by poking his finger in your belly button or runs on by without turning his face and shouts, "That guy with the little tie," "That guy with the little hat," "That guy with the little mustache . . ."

General Cedillo (so very similar to Maxime Weygand) seemed to come from these same depths as General Joaquín Amaro, who left the Yaqui mountains of Sonora, a red kerchief on his head and an earring hanging from one ear, to join the Northwest Division of Álvaro Obregón (a blond young man with blue eyes who, as a child, delivered milk to my maternal grandmother in Alamos) but who, thanks to his beautiful Creole wife, became a polo player and a most elegant martial figure and, by virtue of his own intelligence, the creator of the modern Mexican Army, which emanated from the revolution.

It was from that mold, it seemed to me, that General Cedillo came. He lacked the colorful touches of General Amaro, who had only one eye and spoke impeccable French. But in 1970, it wasn't hard to imagine General Cedillo in the ranks of the revolution. He would have been a very young boy when he joined up, true, but he was also very old because he inherited centuries of refined peasant taciturnity. Diana stared at him, fascinated, admitting without saying so that she didn't understand him. I, thinking I did understand him, kept to myself, ceding to the general a margin of impenetrable mystery but also feeling the writer's inevitable urge: to mock authority.

"Did you have problems with the students in 1968?" I suddenly asked, trying to provoke him.

"The same as everywhere else. It was a movement of discontent that honored the kids who took part in it," he answered, surprisingly.

I felt outflanked by the general and didn't like it one bit.

"They were rebels," I said, "just as you were when you were young, General."

"They'll give it up," he responded, taking the lead I'd

124

involuntarily given him. "He who isn't a rebel as a boy becomes one as an old man. And an old rebel is ridiculous."

He was about to use another, cruder term, but he glanced at Diana and lightly bowed his head, like a mandarin entering a pagoda.

"Was all that blood necessary?" I asked point-blank.

He looked over at the governor's table with a spark of scorn in his eyes. "During the first demonstration, there were those who asked me to call out the troops and put it down. All I said was, Gentlemen, blood's going to flow here, but not yet. Just wait a bit."

"You have to choose the right moment for repression?"

"You have to know when what the people want is order and security, my friend. People get fed up with disorder. The party of stability is the majority party."

That friendly allusion was in itself a challenge, its intent to put me in an inferior position vis-à-vis the man of power. And that power was the power of knowledge, of information. Inwardly, I laughed: first he talked about books and newspapers, only to let me know that true information, the kind that matters when you have to take political action, does not come from what Spaniards call the "black stuff," printed words on paper.

A sumptuous regional dish was served then, interrupting the talk. It was pork rump with *enmoladas*, and I hoped to heaven I would not have to witness the stereotyped reaction on the Yankees' faces—the shock, repugnance, terror, and incredulity. To eat or not to eat? That was the justified dilemma of the gringo in Mexico. I gave Diana a significant look, urging her to try the hot dish, begging her not to succumb to the stereotype. I'd already told her, I eat everything in your country or in my own, and I deal with getting sick there or here. You give a pathetic impression of helplessness when a dish of Mexican food is put in front of you. Why is it that we can have two cultures and you only one, which you comfortably expect to find wherever you go?

Diana tried the *enmoladas*, and next to her the governor laughed as if barking, as he watched the movie star taste the dish that embodied local pride.

"There are people who are novices in politics who get ahead of events and ruin everything," said the general, less circumspectly but with growing scorn. He avoided looking at the governor, though he had to listen to the strange noises the man was making. The sounds could be explained either as culinary euphoria or because that moment the inevitable mariachi band entered, playing their inevitable anthem, the song of the Black Woman. "My little black-skinned sweety, eyes like fluttering paper," intoned the jolly governor.

"But you could have avoided those errors by seizing power," I said provocatively.

"Who do you mean?"

"You. The military."

For the first time, General Cedillo opened his eyes and raised the folds on his forehead where his nonexistent eyebrows should have been.

"Not a chance. Don Benito Juárez would be spinning in his grave."

I remembered the shepherd boy who'd been in the English film.

"Do you mean that the Mexican Army is not the Argentine Army, that you respect republican institutions come what may?"

"I mean that we are an army that emanated from the revolution, a people's army . . ."

"That nevertheless fires on the people if necessary."

"If it's ordered by the constituted authority, civilians," he said without so much as a blink, but I sensed that I'd wounded him, that I'd touched an open sore, that the memory of Tlatelolco was shameful to the army, which wanted to forget the episode and did not speak about it. But at the same time I was to understand what Cedillo was telling me: We only obeyed orders, our honor is intact.

"You shouldn't have done the work of the police or the hawks," I said, and immediately regretted it, not on my account but for my American friends, for Diana. I was breaking my own rule, the one I'd explained to the student Carlos Ortiz: I have no right to compromise them politically.

I was sorry for another reason. By comparing the army to cops and hired assassins, I had insulted it unnecessarily, I thought to myself, just because I was playing around, just because I, too, was a provocateur. But as always happens with me, the more I swore I wouldn't get involved in politics, the more politics got involved with me.

"You were very critical of what happened in '68, I know," he said, wiping the pork-rump sauce off his lips.

"I didn't say even half of what I wanted to," I answered, now out of control, all but foaming at the mouth.

"Tell your girlfriend to be careful," said the Mexican samurai, suddenly transformed into a genuine warlord, owner of the lives gathered that evening around his will, his whim, his mystery.

I couldn't believe my ears. *Tell your girlfriend to be careful?* Is that what the general said? As if to remove any doubts, Cedillo then did what I feared he'd do: he looked at Diana. He stared directly at her, with no disguise, no reticence, a savage glint in his eyes, where I discerned, along with terror,

lust, and death, an instinct tamed for centuries the more easily to leap on its prey, a prey already overwhelmed in that
"right moment" the general had mentioned when we talked
about 1968. He wanted her, he was threatening her, he hated
me—he hated both of us, Diana and me. The commander's
eyes communicated to us in that moment an intense social
hatred, an implacable class opposition, a resentment I felt in
waves, and the intensity of that soldier's stare (usually veiled)
communicated it to the others at the table—the mayor, the
governor, the local bigwigs, the bodyguards. Those brutes
watched Cedillo like people receiving the Host at Communion who feel their bodies and souls full of the Lord. They
stirred, moved around, regrouped, advanced slightly, raised
their hands to the secret guns in their armpits—until the
general's eyelids lowered and the order to stand at ease was
conveyed to them by those eyes so accustomed to giving orders and being obeyed without hesitation, from afar, blindly,
if it came to that.

It was like being caught in a sudden undertow; the tide
went out, the instant of tension went no further, the bodyguards went back to smoking and standing around in Masonic
circles, the governor, the idiot, played the fool, the mayor
ordered the coffee served. But within me the alarm the general aroused continued. His threat hadn't dissipated; I knew
it would be with me, much to my regret, for the rest of my
time in Santiago, screwing up my love, my work, my tran-
quillity . . .

"Don't get involved in anything in Mexico," I told Diana
after I had used her as an excuse to say good-bye. She had a
5:00 a.m. call, so we rose and slowly left the patio. "You get
involved, and you'll never get out of it."

She gave me a determined look, as if I'd insulted her by recommending caution.

I was pleased to see the group of students in a corner of the patio and to realize I could easily tell them apart from the bodyguards. There was no way to confuse the two. Carlos Ortiz was very different from the general and his bodyguards. Knowing the students were different and new saved the evening for me—perhaps they themselves were saved . . . Even so, my anxiety about Diana because of what the general said prevailed over any desire for satisfaction. What did he mean? How could a Hollywood actress bother, interfere with, provoke a general in the Mexican Army?

"Did you sense how heavy the atmosphere was?" I said to Diana.

"Yes. But I didn't understand the reason for it. Did you?"

"No. Me neither."

"We made them jealous because we love each other." Then the woman laughed a beautiful laugh.

"That's it. Yes. No doubt about it."

The words of General Agustín Cedillo reverberated in my head. "Tell your girlfriend to be careful. Whenever you like, come by at two and have lunch with me at the club. Right here in Central Square."

## XX

To respond properly to the gift of the Italian toothpaste and to excuse myself for my attitude toward the shepherd boy, I went out one boring, blazing afternoon to find a present for Diana. The streets of Santiago were abysmally solitary during the afternoon; a leaden sun slammed against the benches, and there were few trees or awnings to provide shade. I felt tired and dizzy after walking ten blocks. I leaned against an ocote-pine-paneled door, and as I did so I caught a glimpse of a cave filled with treasure. It was an antique shop that, for provincial reasons I could not discern, had no sign.

There are restaurants like that in Oaxaca, bookstores in Guadalajara, bars in Guanajuato that don't tell what they are. They believe, I imagine, that advertising isn't needed to lure their clientele. These secret places in Mexico feel that the crowds brought in by publicity would only cheapen the quality of what they offer, and then they would have to satisfy the taste of the least common denominator. The truth is that there is a secret country within Mexico that does not advertise itself, that only tradition knows and recognizes. There, cuisines, legends, memories, conversations—everything that disappears, evaporated, the moment neon light blares it—gestate and continue.

There was lots of turn-of-the-century furniture. Families, when they modernized, when they emigrated from the province to the capital, abandoned these fin de siècle marvels: wicker armchairs, pier glasses, marble-topped dressers, washstands, genre paintings—hunting scenes, still lifes . . . The owner of the shop came over to me. He was a mestizo with slanty eyes, wearing a striped shirt with no collar or tie, although his vest was crossed by a valuable gold watch chain. I smiled and asked if business was going well. "I keep things," he said. "I keep things from turning into dust."

"May I look around?"

"Make yourself at home."

I found an easel piled with posters and badly neglected engravings. I have no idea how posters for the *Normandie*, with its marvelous Art Deco lines, ended up there, even if I could imagine how the ones for the M-G-M films I had seen as a boy in the Iris theater in Mexico City—*Mutiny on the Bounty, The Good Earth, Marie Antoinette*—might have . . .

My fingers touched a sturdy wrinkled paper that had suffered much less than the posters. I smelled or sensed something in that touch and very carefully extracted it from the nest of forgotten colors. It was a Posada. An etching by José Guadalupe Posada, lost in that shop, well preserved, with the printer's address: Antonio Vanegas Arroyo, No. 1 Santa Teresa Street, 1906. I extracted it as if I were in the Albertina in Vienna touching a Lucas Cranach etching. I'm not mistaken in my comparison. There is a relation, distant but certain, between the German painter of the sixteenth century and this artist of the Mexican provinces who died in 1913. They're linked by a long dance of death, a galliard that goes its implacable way, weaving bodies together, day after day adding treasures to humanity's most abundant wealth, death.

Clean, direct, savage, refined, Posada brought a message. A lady dressed in black with a train to her skirt, revolver in hand, had just murdered another lady, also dressed in black with a train to her skirt and also with a pistol in her hand. Obviously, the first lady had gotten the drop on the second. But the murderess had turned her back on an open balcony and to the light of the sun, as if the promise of her crime were, despite everything, life. The murdered woman, on the other hand, was imprisoned by a serpent whose coils were suffocating her, making the viewer doubt whether in fact she'd been murdered by her presumptive rival or whether Posada was depicting—as he did in other pictures, with a serpent wrapped tightly around a woman's body, braiding her—an epileptic.

In any case, behind her opened the jaws of a devouring toothy monster that in fact was the entrance to a circus. Flying out of that open mouth were bats and demons, souls in torment, succubi and incubi: a whole carnival of malignant dreams, a nightmare that transformed the murder of an elegant woman dressed in black into one that would be its double, a Mardi Gras of sickness, death, laughter, gambling, news, all mixed together . . .

The little man with the golden chain asked so little money that I was about to give him twice as much, as a gift. I didn't, because he would have taken offense. I waited until after dinner to give my present to Diana. But she was tired that night and fell asleep early. I read for a while and then followed her. Tomorrow I'd give her the present. Then I woke up with a shock, and she was sitting next to me, trembling.

"Diana, what's the matter?"

"I was dreaming."

I looked at her in silence. She told me this: A woman dressed in black shot her to death. Diana, also dressed in black, was falling, mortally wounded, though the instantaneous death was accompanied by convulsions.

"What else?"

"That's all."

"Wasn't there a snake wrapped around you?"

"What are you talking about? The most important thing, I want you to know, was the sky, a little piece of sky that you could see through the window."

"The murderess had her back to the open balcony."

"How do you know?"

Diana's dream upset me so much that I made the mistake of going too far, of asking her if there was also, behind her, a horrible mouth filled with vampires.

"No. Not even that snake around me. You can skip the Freud for Beginners, okay? I told you I don't want a biographical chicken with Freudian dressing. I told you that before. When you hear someone say 'poor country girl devoured by instant success,' don't believe it. Don't believe the story of the innocent girl abused by the tyrannical Teutonic director. Only believe in the images of me that you take away from our relationship."

"You yourself give me so many, I don't have to invent anything."

"Then don't believe anything about me."

# XXI

I decided not to play along with her irrational manias—the bathroom door always closed, the window curtains always open in expectation of moonlight pouring in on a snowy landscape. Her accusation annoyed me: "You have no imagination." Actually, what I wanted was for us to share the imagination of the future instead of that morbid imagination of a past in which I didn't figure. There was pride in that, but also fear, fear that Diana's memory would enslave me and that we would both lose in a morbid reconstruction of irrecoverable moments.

It seemed strange to me to be in such a position, a Mexican supposedly loaded down with too much past, she a midwestern gringa supposedly devoid of memory. Was that why she wanted to invent for herself a treasure chest of memories, a true mnemonic treasure, inviting me to re-create it with her? No doubt about it. But at that moment I was living through a crisis of power with regard to women, a crisis precipitated by vanity and caprice. It excluded the vanity and caprice of women, eliminated them and occasionally eliminated the women, too, if they didn't obey my desire for them to eliminate their own caprices.

Once I went to Taxco with a rich Mexican girl who complained about the hotel room. It seemed too low-class to her. I told her she was an intolerable rich brat, incapable of adapting to circumstances and devoid of fantasy or the spirit of adventure, but what I was really saying was: Just count yourself lucky that I actually brought you along for the weekend. I decided no Mexican woman was going to gain power over me through whim, vanity, pride. I'd always be one step ahead of them; I'd give them a dose of their own medicine. They'd hurt me too much when I was young. They were weak, vain, easy to convince when their parents crossed me off the eligible-bachelor list just because I had no money and my rivals did. Now that they were after me, I paid them back in kind, knowing all along that I was hurting myself more than I was hurting them. By denying Diana that share of her imagination which she demanded, I was letting myself be swept along by the inertia of my previous loves. She was no spoiled Mexican brat, and I was committing a serious error with an exceptional woman.

I quickly tried to make up for it, letting her know that I would bow to her desire to close the bathroom door and to imagine a snowy moonlit night. She was puzzled by my attitude, annoyed sometimes. She begged me to close the door. But she berated me scornfully for not helping her recover her lost imagination. That confirmed for me a basic Hispano-Arab conviction: in the harem it is not the eunuch who rules but the sultan. Diana would become terribly weak and sweet when she begged me please to leave the bathroom door closed, and I would feel guilty for not acceding to her wish.

135

Perhaps I saw in her pleas something that always annoyed the hell out of me: someone giving me orders, especially orders about order.

I always had a good relationship with my father, a very good relationship, except on that one point. I loved to infuriate him with my disorder. He was the son of a German woman and was proud of his punctuality, his refined devotion to order. His closets, his papers, and his schedule were all examples of a well-ordered life. I piled papers on my desk, left my dirty shirts on the floor, and one day, right before his eyes, I put on my shoes and then tugged and pulled my trousers over them. The spectacle horrified and disgusted him. But it also aroused a tenderness in him I would never have expected. He saw my weakness. He accepted it. He forgave me. He never again gave me an order, and I never again took one from anybody. I organized my life around my work so as to be independent or, in any case, to choose my dependencies with a certain freedom. And my physical disorder became a motive for mental order. In the chaos of my work papers, books, and letters, I always know—and only I know—where things are. As if I had radar in my head, my hand shoots directly to the Leaning Tower of Paper and instantly finds exactly what it seeks. Sometimes the tower collapses, but the object is never lost.

Emotions, unlike papers, refuse to be catalogued in order or disorder. They challenge us to find their form—only to disappear like the perfume of certain flowers that seems to be the most fixed, the most real thing in the world and yet has no more form than the rose or iris from which it emanates. We know, of course, that the form of the rose is not its scent, but in effect, its scent is a phantom similar to emotions, which are the realest but least apprehensible things in the world. I punished myself mentally for my mistakes in dealing with a woman like Diana Soren, allowing myself to slide on the little sled of my domestic loves. I convinced myself that she was giving me passion and tenderness, and I was too lucky not to realize the privilege it was to love her, even if that meant giving in, if necessary, to her whims and imaginings.

Another night, she woke up agitated. She told me she'd imagined herself entering a salon she expected to find full of people. From far off, she could hear the conversations, the laughter, the music, even the tinkle of glasses. But when she walked in, no one was there. She heard only the rustle of a long skirt, as of taffeta. She began to shout so she'd be heard outside. She woke; I thought about the Posada I'd given her.

# XXII

Diana's whims and nocturnal frights lulled me into inattention. If I heard her stirring at night, I ignored it. If she got out of bed, still half asleep I would imagine her opening curtains and closing doors. When she appeared in my dreams, she was wearing black, standing opposite a balcony while another woman, identically dressed, shot her.

But there was no music in this catalog of grotesque images. Everything occurred during long silences punctuated by the shots. One night Diana's voice, far off and odd, was chanting something in a voice that wasn't her own, as if another, far-off, maybe even dead voice had come back to possess hers, taking advantage of the night to recover a presence lost in oblivion, death, the usury of time.

The sensation was so strange, so alarming that I focused all my attention on it, clearing the cobwebs from my head to hear and see her clearly. That night the full moon was indeed pouring in through the open window like a huge white embrace: Diana was sitting next to it wearing her white baby-dolls, whispering a song I soon identified. It was one of Tina Turner's early hits, a song called "Remake Me" or "Make Me Over."

Diana had something in her hands; she was singing to an object. Of course—the telephone, I admitted with pain and instant jealousy, banishing the image of a woman perturbed by the full moon, a forlorn she-wolf howling to the goddess of the night: Artemis, her nemesis; Diana, her namesake.

If the flash of pain told me first that she was insane, the stab of jealousy quickly put me on notice: she was singing to someone ... Should I break up this melodrama with a scene of my own, a jealous, furious scene? Caution overcame honor, and curiosity prevailed over both. Neither Hamlet nor Othello, that night I was just Prometheus's brother Epimetheus, interested more in knowing what was happening than in stopping or ignoring it. If I didn't proceed carefully, I'd never know what was going on ... I opened Pandora's box.

I pretended to be asleep. I stopped listening to her. After a while, I felt her warm body next to mine, but it was strangely distant and she didn't feel around with her feet for mine that night, as she did on others ...

How long could I control my desire to know to whom Diana was talking at three in the morning, to whom she was singing Tina Turner songs over the telephone? Because, beginning that night, she talked every night, sitting in a pool of light shed by the waning moon, in a distant and at first incomprehensible voice (another voice, imitated or possessive; Diana, owner of a mimic's voice, or the mimic's voice possessing Diana, I don't know which) that became louder as the moon died, more audible, passing from the lyrics of "Remake Me" to sentences not sung but spoken in that same deep, velvety voice, which wasn't Diana's. Her normal voice came from above, from her clear eyes, or maybe even from her lovely soft white breasts; this nocturnal voice came from her guts, her ovaries, maybe even from her solar plexus. She was saying things I couldn't understand without knowing the question or answer to which they were directed on the other end of the line, wherever that might be . . .

I remembered the Capitano toothpaste sent from Italy and imagined long-distance communication with who knows what place on the globe. Impossible to guess; all I heard, with ever-increasing unease, was Diana's different voice and the inexplicable words "Who takes care of me?"

I knew it sure wasn't me. She wasn't asking me to take care of her. But she was asking someone else, maybe more than one someone else. A lover, her parents, her husband, with whom she maintained a close and affectionate relationship (three in the morning in Mexico, midday in Paris)? But I knew that the woman talking wasn't Diana. She said it clearly. One night she was saying, I'm Tina; another, I'm Aretha; another I'm Billie . . . I understood the allusions, in retrospect. Billie Holiday was the Our Lady of Sorrows of jazz singers, our voice of every grief, the voice which we dare not listen to in ourselves but which she takes on in our name, like a black, feminine Christ, a crucified Christ to bear all our sins:

*Got the moon above me*
*But no one to love me*
*Lover man, where can you be?*

140

Aretha Franklin was the joyful voice of the soul, the grand, collective ceremony of redemption, a renewed, purifying baptism that peels off our used-up, worn-out names and gives us new ones, clean and shining.

*A woman's only human, you've got to understand.*

And Tina Turner was the woman abused, wounded, victimized by society, prejudice, machismo; the young woman who, no matter what, felt in her subjugation the promise of a free, clear maturity that would fill the world with joy because she'd known great sorrows.

*You might as well face it:*
*You're addicted to love.*

Between the songs, I listened to phrases that had no meaning for me—they weren't part of a well-known song, recorded and repeated by everyone—garbled chunks of a dialogue that for me was Diana's monologue in the moonlight.
"How? I'm white."
What was being said to her? What was she answering, what was being asked? What did Diana mean when she said into the phone, "Make me see myself as another woman"? These questions began to torture me because of their intrinsic mystery, because of the distance the mystery created between my lover and me, because my obsession with knowing what was going on, whom Diana was speaking with, interrupted my mornings, kept me from working, plunged me into a literary depression. Reluctantly I revised my pages and found them lifeless, mechanical, devoid of the passion and enigma of my possible daily life: Diana was my enigma, but I myself was becoming an enigma to myself. Both of us were only possibilities.

I would wait impatiently for night and the mystery.

I didn't dare, from the bed, interrupt Diana's secret dialogue. It would only cause a scene, perhaps a complete break. Once again, I confessed to myself that I was a coward when faced with the idea of losing my adored lover. I'd gain nothing by getting out of bed, going over to her, grabbing the telephone from her hand, and demanding, like some husband in a melodrama, Who are you talking to, who are you cheating on me with?

I humiliated myself by searching through Diana's things to see if I could find a name written down by chance, a telephone number, a letter, any clue about her mysterious nocturnal interlocutor. I felt dirty, small, despicable, opening drawers, handbags, suitcases, zippers, slipping my fingers like dark worms through panties, stockings, brassieres, all the indescribable lingerie that once had dazzled me and that now I was handling as if it were old rags, Kleenex to be thrown out, soiled Kotex . . .

She had to give me the chance I needed. One night, she did. She invited me, I'm sure of it, to share her mystery.

# XXIII

The old actor was depressed that night, conjuring up memories and longing, paradoxically, for a past time that had abandoned him. He felt betrayed by his time. He also felt he'd betrayed something—the promise, the optimism of the New Deal years. In his evocation of names, literary works, and organizations of the 1930s, there was both nostalgia and disdain, yes, a disdainful nostalgia. He said to himself and to us; There were so many promises that were not carried out. To himself and to us he said, We didn't deserve to see them carried out.

That night he would have wanted to channel that feeling into one of the parlor games with which we blocked out the tedium of Santiago. Since he got no answer from Diana or me (both of us tightly sealed—she certainly knew I was, and I knew she was—in the enigma of those nocturnal telephone calls, always furtive, never mentioned by light of day), Lew Cooper launched into an unsolicited explanation of why he

143

had named names to the House Un-American Activities Committee. He was precise and forcefully persuasive.

"No one deserved respect. Neither the members of the committee nor the members of the Communist Party. Both seemed despicable to me. Both trafficked in lies. Why should I sacrifice myself for either side? To save my honor? By dying of hunger? I wasn't a cynic—don't even think that. I simply behaved the way all of them behaved, the fascists on the right who interrogated me or the fascists on the left who never lifted a finger for me. I was selective, that's true. I never gave them the name of anyone who was weak, anyone who could be hurt. I was selective. I only gave the names of those who would have treated me in Moscow exactly the way these people were treating me in Washington. They deserved one another. Why should I be the sacrificial lamb in their mutual dirty tricks?"

"Can you measure the damage you might have done to those you didn't want to hurt?" I asked.

"I didn't mention them. Other people did. Lives were destroyed, but I didn't destroy them. The only thing I did was not destroy myself. I admit it."

"The bad thing about the United States is that if you're denounced as anti-patriotic everyone believes it. In the U.S.S.R., on the other hand, no one would believe it. Vyshinsky had no credibility; McCarthy did."

I said that, but Diana quickly added, "My husband always says that the dilemma of liberals in America is that they have an enormous sense of injustice but no sense of justice. They denounce, but they do nothing."

"I read that," I said. "He goes on to say that they refuse to face the consequences of their acts."

Was that the moment to ask her, calmly, if the person

144

she'd been speaking to at night was her husband? What if it wasn't? Would I be opening a can of worms? Once again, I remained silent. The old actor was going on about the extraordinary excitement of the stage experiments of the Group Theatre in New York, the communion between the audience and the actors during the 1930s, the time and the scene of my own youth . . .

The barrier between stage and audience disappeared. The people in the audience were also actors and were totally enraptured by those extraordinary performances, never realizing the terrible illusion they were sharing with the actors on stage. The tragedies represented by the actors would sadly and painfully become the tragedies lived by the audience. And the actors, part of society, after all, wouldn't escape the destiny they first acted out. Frances Farmer, blond as a wheat field, ended up tainted by alcohol, prostitution, madness, and fire. John Garfield, master of all the urban rage there ever was, died making love.

"Don't you envy him?" Diana interrupted.

"J. Edward Bromberg, Clifford Odets, Gale Sondergaard— all persecuted, mutilated, burned by witch-hunters . . ."

"Odets was married to a woman of sublime beauty, Luise Rainer," I recalled. "A Viennese advertised as the Eleonora Duse of our time. Why Duse? Why not just herself—Luise Rainer, the incomparable, fragile, fainting, passionate Luise Rainer, wounded by the world because she wanted to be . . . ?"

"*Someone else*," said Diana. "Don't you get it? She wanted to be someone else—Duse, Bernhardt, anyone but herself . . ."

"You're speaking for yourself," I dared to blurt out.

"For every actress," said Diana, vehement and exasperated.

"Naturally, every actress wants to be someone else, otherwise she wouldn't be an actress," said Lew avuncularly.

"No," said Diana, her eyes wide with fright, "more than that. To refuse to take on the parts they assign you, to take on instead characters you've only heard talked about . . ."

Right then and there I repeated her words, personalizing them, rooting them in her, taking away the disguise of the infinitive ("to be or not to be") and that impersonal "you" Americans use. *You* refuse to take on the parts they give *you*. *You* interpret characters that *you've* only heard talked about . . .

I said all that to avoid saying what I really wanted to: Whom were you talking to on the telephone at three in the morning? My rage simply took twisted paths. The actor felt the tension between us rising above his own, so he went on with his evocation.

"I heard Luise Rainer say something very beautiful to Clifford Odets. She said she was born prematurely, so she was always searching for the two months she missed. Then she said, I found them with you. But he was a left-wing radical and rewrote her words: The general strike gave me the two months I was missing. Not love but the strike. The truth is, we're all looking for the months we're missing. Two. Or nine. It's all the same. We want more. We want to be someone else. Diana's right . . . Odets sacrificed his wife to coin a political slogan."

"Diana wants to disguise herself and to disguise us." I laughed sarcastically, offensively. "She invited you to live here to disguise our little affair. Even if it's a fact and everyone knows it, she must disguise it, you see, so as to act, to be someone else, to be a good actress in life because she can't

146

be a good one on screen . . . I hate whores who want to be seen as bourgeois housewives."

"Good night," said Lew, getting up abruptly and looking at me with disdain.

"No. Don't leave yet. Don't you know that you and I are living here in a monastery with Diana, you the father superior, I the novice? Or could it be some kind of artistic utopia, you the minstrel, I the scribe, Azucena the sluttish maid. But no one fornicates here—not a chance. Who ever heard of that? People come here to take refuge, they don't take refuge here to come. Filthy convent, crummy utopia . . ."

"I'd rather listen to rock and roll, which I loathe, than to this stupid litany. Good night, Diana."

"Good night, Lew," she said, her eyes anxious but resigned.

I parodied her in falsetto. "Oh dear, oh dear! Why did I ever invite these people to share my house?"

"Come to bed, sweetheart. You've had a lot to drink today."

147

# XXIV

She was right, and it was hard for me to fall asleep. I understood everything. That night she got up. Ostentatiously she did not turn to see if I was asleep. She left the bedroom. The curtains were open. The moonlight fell freely on the old black telephone. I heard a light click. I got up, walked to the lunar pool. I held out my hand to take the telephone. I stopped out of fear. Would she realize I knew? Was she talking at that very moment from another part of the house? Did I have the right to listen in on a private conversation? I'd already pawed through bags, drawers, lingerie . . . What would one more indignity matter?

I picked up the telephone and heard the two voices talking on the extension. Hers was the unknown voice I'd learned to recognize at night, in secret. A voice that came from a different geography, another age, to take control of hers . . . that was my fantasy. Actually, it was just the voice of the actress Diana Soren acting a part she'd never be given in a film. The voice of a black woman. She was talking with a black man. That was clear. Even if it was a white man imitating a black, just as she was imitating a black woman, it was a black man's voice. I mean it was the voice of someone who wanted to be black, only black. That impressed me, blowing away the alcoholic mist of my growing bitterness (as the tango—or is it the bolero?—goes . . . ). Now I understood what I had heard in the bedroom, the previous nights, when she said things like "Make me see myself as another woman" or "How? I'm white."

"Make yourself black."

"How? I'm white."

"You'll figure out how."

"I'm trying hard."

"No, Aretha. Don't be stupid. I'm not asking you to change the color of your skin. You understand what I mean."

"I want to be with you," said Diana, transformed into Aretha. "I'd give anything to be with you, in your bed . . ."

"You can't, baby, you're in your cage. I already got out of mine . . ."

"I'm not talking about a cage, I'm talking about a bed, with both of us in it . . ."

"Set us free, Aretha. Free the black man who doesn't want a white woman, because he'd be betraying his mother. Free the white man who doesn't want a black woman, because he'd be betraying his prejudices. Free the black man who wants a white woman to avenge his father. Free the white man who wants a black woman to humiliate, abandon, make a slave even in pleasure. Do all that, baby, and then I'll be yours . . ."

"I'll try to change my soul, if that's what you want, dar-ling."

"You can't."

"Why? Don't—"

The black man hung up but Diana sat there listening to the telephone static. I quickly hung up and went back to bed, feeling horribly guilty. But the next night I couldn't resist the temptation to go on listening to the interrupted but eternal conversation, night after night . . .

She told him she'd try to change her soul, and he said, You can't. She begged him not to condemn her that way, not to be unjust, but he insisted, You can't. At heart you think we want to be white—that's why you'll never be able to be black. Diana Soren said she wanted justice for all. She reminded the black man she was against racism, she'd marched, she'd demonstrated; he knew it. Why didn't he accept her as an equal? His burst of laughter must have wakened all the sleeping birds between Los Angeles and Santiago. You want them to let us into country clubs, he said to Diana, into luxury hotels, into McDonald's, but we don't want to get in. We want them to keep us out, we want them to do us the favor of telling us, Don't come in, you're different, we hate you, you smell bad, you're ugly, you look like monkeys, you're stupid, you're not like us. He was gasp-ing for breath and said that every time a liberal, philan-thropic white spoke against racism he felt like castrating him and making him eat his own balls.

"I don't want to be like you whites. I don't want to be like you!"

The next night, she told him she only wanted to see her-self as another woman so she could see herself as she really was. Everyone had his objective—he had his, and she had hers . . .

"Respect me. After all, I'm an actress, not a politician . . ."

The man burst into laughter again.

"Then dedicate yourself to your thing and don't play with fire, asshole. But let's get something straight. Nobody can see himself as he is unless he sees himself separated, divorced from the human race, radically separated, a leper, alone, with his own kind . . ."

Almost crying, she told him she couldn't, that what he wanted was impossible, and he insulted her—You cunt, you fucking white cunt—and she gave something like a sigh of joy . . .

"You'd have to be pure black, a black from Africa before he was brought here, before mixing, and not even then could you live separated . . ."

"Shut up, Aretha. Shut up, whore . . ."

Triumphantly, Diana told him there were no pure blacks in America; they were all descended from whites as well . . . "I'm not saying that to offend you. I'm saying it so you'll think you share something with me . . ."

"Shut up, whore. You don't have a drop of black blood, you don't have a mulatto child . . ."

She said she'd like to give in to that temptation, but of her own free will, not to prove a point. "I don't want to use my sex to win arguments."

"Whore, white cunt . . ."

He called her the next night to ask forgiveness. He tried to explain himself with a humility that seemed suspicious to me. He told her that she wanted to change the system.

Then he added, in humble scorn, in the voice of Little Black Sambo, How good you are, how compassionate, and how hypocritical. She had to understand that the system doesn't change, he said, slowly but surely recovering his normal aggressive tone; the system has to be smashed. She was silent, didn't get the joke, then said, honestly and with sincere emotion, that she wanted to help them. "But I don't think I know how . . ."

"You can begin by not reminding me I'm a mulatto."

"But you are. I like you like that. I love you like that. Doesn't that matter to you?"

She should tell him that he, too, was going to give in to temptation, like his ancestors, that he, too, was going to fall for a white slut, that he, too, was going to have a mulatto child with her. What did she think of that? Would she honestly accept it? Wouldn't she run around screaming, not her, she wasn't promiscuous, it was a lie, she would never have children that weren't Aryan, white, Nordic . . . ?

"Me, I'm going to insult all the blacks." Now the absent mulatto was speaking with a voice like a sea in chains. "All the blacks that should have stayed African and who betrayed their race giving in to temptation and screwing a white woman and having café-au-lait children. Say that, whore. Think that, give me that slap. No matter how far away you are, Aretha, I swear I'm going to feel your slap. It'll hurt even more because you're far away, screwing a white man. I can see you from here. There's not enough distance between California and Mexico for me not to see you or smell your blond cunt and spit on it . . ."

"Don't mention names, don't say names . . ."

"Don't be a jerk. They know everything. They tape everything. Are you out of your head?"

"I'm Aretha. My name is Aretha."

"Make yourself black."

"How? I'm white."

"You'll figure out how to do it. I can't accept you if you don't."

"I'll call you tomorrow."

"Okay. Fuck off, bitch."

The next night was the last call. He spoke very calmly and said that Diana's error was to think everyone was guilty, including her, including the oppressors. If that were so, they'd all be innocent. No, only the kids who didn't leave the ghetto were oppressed, the drug-addict mothers, the fathers forced to steal, the men castrated by the Klan—those were the oppressed, not the poor oppressors.

"Know how you can make yourself black, Aretha? Have you figured out that in this country the only crimes people get convicted for committing are crimes committed by blacks? Have you realized that black victims never arouse compassion, only white ones? That's what I'm asking you to do, Aretha: make yourself into a black victim and you'll see how they throw you into the street like a dog so the trucks roll over you and turn you into a bloody, rotten chunk of meat. Commit a crime as a black and pay for it as a black. Be a victim as a black so nobody feels sorry for you."

The black started laughing and crying at the same time. My hand was shaking, but I hung up carefully and returned to bed before she did, as I had all the other nights. I pretended to be asleep. Diana counted on my deep sleep and the stupor of the hangover I'd have in the morning. She came back in and got into bed silently. I could sense that she fell asleep immediately, content, relieved, as if nothing satisfied her more than this nightly exchange of insults, passions, and guilt.

Eyes open, prisoner of the ceiling of this suddenly frozen bedroom, a faded battleground, I repeated to myself over and over, like someone counting sheep, that my passion was nothing compared with those I'd just heard, that having listened to the passion of Diana and her black I should accept that my own was a passing fancy, and that perhaps the honorable thing to do was to give up this arrangement, turn my back on Diana, and go back to my life in Mexico City.

But in the course of that night's insomnia, which diminished my own passion considerably, another certainty asserted itself little by little, involuntarily, an idea that was part of me though I hadn't formulated it clearly. I was sorry, I said to myself. Both within myself and in the outside world, I saw manifested the idea that civilized life respects laws while savage life disdains them. I didn't want to say it or even think it, because it contradicted or, in its own way, disparaged the sorrow I could feel in the rage of Diana's black lover. Yet despite that, I was as repelled by the idea of black supremacy as of white supremacy. I couldn't put myself in the shoes of that unknown interlocutor. I didn't need to tell Diana I couldn't jive, didn't swing to black street rhythms . . .

I wanted to be sincere and to imagine myself, on the other hand, in the sandals of that boy who'd played the part of Juárez. Would I have helped the boy Juárez? Would I have helped him become what he became—a white Indian, a Zapotec with the Napoleonic Code for his pillow, a Cartesian lawyer, a Republican shyster instead of a shaman, a paper pusher instead of a sorcerer in contact with nature and death, animator of the inanimate, owner of things that cannot be possessed, millionaire of misery? What would I have done for the boy Juárez?

Nothing. Diana's black—her Panther, I decided to call him—knew me better than I knew him and maybe even better than I knew myself. He knew that I could take everything away from him whenever I wanted. Everything. The castrated, hanged, lynched blacks, like milestones in American history— they are also a book of martyrs for innocent blacks. The Panther decided he would no longer be the victim. God never stopped the homicidal hand of the white Abraham when he sank his dagger into the heart of his son, the black Isaac.

# XXV

I had a bad morning, but at lunchtime I decided to visit the club and see if General Agustín Cedillo was there, as he was every day. In the old-fashioned way, he was drinking a cognac before lunch and invited me to sit with him. I had a beer instead of a cognac because no beer in the world is better than ours. It made me feel rather chauvinist, but I was thankful for that feeling. I remembered what Diana had told me James Baldwin said—that a black and a white, because they're both Americans, know more about themselves and one another than any European knows about either of them. The same thing is true of Mexicans.

The other night I had felt class hatred flare up between the general and me. This afternoon the beer raised my spirits and made me recognize myself in him. In one voice we both ordered "two Tehuacans," knowing well that in no other part of the world would anyone understand what that mineral water was. Then he invited me to join him. The ritual of dining—from ordering *quesadillas* with *huitlacoche* (only we Mexicans understand and enjoy eating the black cancer of corn) to being handed a basket of hot tortillas and delicately picking one out, spreading guacamole on it, adding a dash of chile, and rolling it all up; from the diminutive and possessive references to all edibles (your little beans, your little chiles, your little tortillas) to the guarded, familiar, tender allusions to health, weather, age (he's not well, the rain's letting up, he's getting so elderly)—created a favorable climate for bringing up the theme that concerned me. It also allowed me to free myself, in an involvement the general knew nothing of, from the extreme alienation, still buzzing in my ears, of that pair Diana Soren and her Panther. They were other. But everything at the table was Mexican, right down to my possessive when I addressed General Cedillo: My general, my general, dear, oh dear. That was it: he was mine.

"You said the other night that my girlfriend should be careful. Why?"

"Look, my friend, I'm not a professional suspicion monger. I don't go around seeing enemies behind every tree. But the fact is, here and there agitators do exist. You understand me. We wouldn't want Miss Soren to find herself compromised for an indiscretion."

"Do you mean Black Panthers there and the League guerrillas here?"

"Not exactly. I mean FBI everywhere, that's what I mean. Watch out."

"What do you suggest I do?"

"You're a friend of the gentleman who runs the Department of Internal Affairs."

"You mean Mario Moya Palencia. We went to school together. He's an old, close friend."

"Go visit him in Mexico City. Be careful. Watch out for your girlfriend. It's not worth the trouble."

When Diana came back that night, I told her I'd be leaving for Mexico City the next day. I had to attend to some unfinished business. She knew I'd left everything hanging in midair to follow her to Santiago. In a few days, a week at the most, I'd be back. She looked at me with a melancholy expression, trying to guess the truth, imagining that perhaps I'd guessed the truth about her but laying open a range of possibilities. How much did I know? Was this the end? Was I leaving for good? Was this the end of our relationship? Was I being drawn back by my wife, my daughter, my business in the capital?

"I'm leaving everything here—my books, my papers, my typewriter . . ."

"Take the toothpaste with you."

Nothing lessened the sadness in her eyes.

"Just one tube. Everything else stays in the pawnshop."

"In the pawnshop? I like that. Maybe all of us are only in the pawnshop here."

"Don't start imagining God as some Jewish pawnbroker."

"No. But I do believe in God. So much, you know, that I can't imagine He put us on earth just to be no one."

"I love you, Diana." I kissed her.

# XXVI

The first thing I did when I got back to Mexico City was to call my friend Luis Buñuel and ask to see him. Once or twice a month I'd visit him between four and six in the afternoon. His conversation nourished and stimulated me in extraordinary ways. Buñuel not only had witnessed the century (they were coevals—he was born in 1900) but had been one of its greatest creators. Everyone knows that, even as they demand automatic writing and a "disordering of the senses," the French theoreticians of surrealism have given us beautiful essays and other texts written with Cartesian clarity. Beyond mere provocation, the French Surrealists seem not to compromise their rationalist culture or to give it back that blast of madness that must have animated Villon or Rabelais. But the Surrealists without theory, the intuitive ones like Buñuel in Spain or Max Ernst in Germany, succeed in incorporating their culture into their art, giving the past a critical presence and placing historically perverse limits on modern pretensions to novelty. Everything is rooted in distant memories and ancient soil. Dig them up and true modernity bursts forth: the presence of the past, a warning against the pride of progress. The Spanish mystics, the picaresque novel, Cervantes, and Goya were the fathers of Buñuel's surrealism, just as the cruel, excessive nocturnal fantasy of the Germanic fairy tale was mother to Ernst.

Buñuel's house in Colonia del Valle lacked all character. That, in effect, was its character: it had none. A two-story red brick building, it looked like any middle-class house in the world. The living room resembled a dentist's waiting room, and although I never saw the artist's bedroom, I know he liked to look at bare walls and to sleep on the floor or, at most, on a wooden bed with no mattress or springs. Those penances fit nicely with his strict morality, oppressively bourgeois and puritanical for some, ascetically monastic for others. His house was almost devoid of decoration, except for a portrait of Buñuel as a young man painted by Dalí in the 1920s. Since World War II they'd been enemies, but Luis kept the portrait in his vestibule as a heartfelt homage to his youth and also to a lost friendship . . .

He'd receive guests around a liquor cabinet in a room equipped with a real bar he'd bought at the Liverpool department store around the corner. It was as well stocked as the Oak Room at the Plaza Hotel in New York—the place where Buñuel liked to drink the "best martinis in the world," as he put it. Now he was mixing up a *buñueloni* for me, a delicious but intoxicating mixture of gin, Carpano, and Angostura, and proclaiming, "I drink a liter of alcohol every day. Alcohol's going to kill me."

"But you look very well," I said, admiring his robust physique at the age of seventy, his well-rounded shoulders, his powerful chest, and his arms, strong but thin.

"I just saw the doctor. Here's the list: I've got emphysema, diverticulosis, high cholesterol, and a gigantic prostate. If I deal with them one at a time, I'm in perfect shape. But if they all gang up on me, I'll drop dead."

Generally, he wore short-sleeved sport shirts, which accentuated the bareness of his peasant-philosopher head. His baldness and his face creased by time made him look like Picasso, de Falla, Ortega y Gasset. Illustrious Spaniards end up looking like retired picadors. Buñuel came from the same region as Goya, from Aragon, a famous breeding ground of stubborn individuals. The truth is that no one dreams more than the Aragonese. Their wild dreams are about witches' Sabbaths and communication between men, animals, and insects. Everyone knows that ants are the beings that communicate among themselves best—telepathically, over huge distances—and I think Luis Buñuel had a passion for entomology because the Aragonese, like ants, communicate with one another across space and time. They're in contact through their nightmares, their witches, their drums.

He wasn't pleased with me that afternoon. He was a confirmed believer in matrimonial fidelity and in the inviolability of man and wife. It seemed intolerable to him that a couple, having made a pact to live together, should break it. He reproached me openly for abandoning Luisa Guzmán, whom he loved a lot and whom he'd used in one or two of his pictures. But along with that exaltation of the bonds of matrimony, Buñuel did not hide his horror of the sexual act. It was rare in his pictures to see a naked person, except as a necessary counterpoint to the plot; there was never a kiss, which seemed an "indecency" to him, and never fornication, only desire, rolling around in the gardens of the Golden Age, desire forever unsatisfied so as to maintain the flame of passion at its highest intensity.

I looked at his green eyes, as distant as a sea I'd never sailed, and through them I saw sail the ship of Tristan, Buñuel's secret hero, the hero of chaste, unconsummated love. The Middle Ages was Buñuel's real era, his natural time, and it was there his gaze navigated; he was accidentally anchored in our "detestable time." He had to be seen and understood as someone exiled from the past, a foreigner from the thirteenth century almost naked among us, dressed in a short-sleeved sport shirt like a hermit monk given only a loincloth to cover his shame.

It was from that lost era that Buñuel got the idea he was repeating to me now—of sex as a habit of animals, *more bestiarum*, in the words of Saint Augustine. "Sex," he was saying, "is a hairy spider, an all-devouring tarantula, a black hole from which you never emerge if you give in to it." He was deaf (again, like Goya) and had abandoned the use of music in his pictures unless it fit in naturally: a radio, an organ grinder, an orchestra at a ski resort. Before, he'd filled his movies with the infinitely impassioned, sweet, stormy refrains of Wagner's *Liebestraum*. The music of *Tristan and Isolde* was the cantata to chaste love from which the tarantulas of sex have been expelled.

"But Saint John Chrysostom prohibited even chaste love, saying it succeeded only in making passion greater, adding more flames to desire," I recalled.

"Well, now, don't you see why it's the most exciting thing in the world? Sex without sin is like an egg without salt."

I always fell into his trap. Buñuel preached chastity as the means to augment pleasure, desire, the thirst for the amatory body. He was a reader of Saint Augustine and understood that the Fall only meant that the law of love had been broken. Love has a law, which is to love God. To love ourselves is to break the law of God and start down the road of perdition, which wends lower and lower through the black hole of sex to the final hole of death. To return to love means to pass through chastity, but for that we need help. We can't do it alone. To return to God from the hell of flesh and its self-gratification is like defying the law of gravity. Not falling but flying.

"Who's going to help us?" I asked.

"Not power," he said passionately. "Never those wielding power, whether it's civil or ecclesiastic. Only the poor, the rebels, the outcasts, children, lovers . . . only those can help us."

He said all this with great emotion, and through my memory paraded the abandoned children of his movies, the ardent couples, the damned beggars, the priests humiliated because of their Christian devotion, all those who renounced the vanity of this world and hoped only for the embrace of a brother. Rebels, too? I asked Buñuel. Rebels help us as well?

"If they don't obey any power," Luis answered. "If they are totally gratuitous."

At the time, Buñuel was working on a script for a film he never made, based on the story of the French anarchist Ravachol, who started out as a thief and a murderer. Back in the provinces, he had killed an old ragman and an elderly hermit, violated the grave of a countess, and stabbed to death two spinsters who owned a forge. All that was gratuitous. But one fine day he declared that he'd stolen the hermit's and the spinster's money and the jewels buried with the countess for the sake of the anarchist cause.

Even so, the anarchists did not give him their blessing until Ravachol moved to Paris and, with an assistant named Simon the Biscuit, dedicated himself to making bombs he placed at judges' doors. Unfortunately, the Biscuit confused doors, and it wasn't the judges who died but some innocent passers-by. That in itself, observed Buñuel, gave a fantastic gratuitousness to the whole thing.

Only when Ravachol was executed on July 11, 1892, did the anarchists claim him as one of their own, canonizing him and even coining a verb, "to ravacholize," which means to explode into pieces which inspired a cute song that goes something like *"Dansons la ravachole. Vive le son de l'explosion!"*

"When he ascended the gallows, he shouted, Long live anarchism! He was a bastard and used rouge to cover the pallor of his cheeks."

"Do you approve of him, Luis?"

"Yes, in theory."

"What does that mean?"

"That anarchism is marvelous as an idea of freedom—you have no one above you. No superior power, no chains. There isn't an idea more marvelous than that. There isn't one less practicable, either. But we've got to maintain the utopia of ideas. If we don't, we become animals. Practical life is also a black hole that leads us to death. Revolution, anarchy, and freedom are the prizes of thought. The only throne they have is in our heads."

He went on to say that there was no more beautiful idea than blowing up the Louvre and telling humanity and all its

164

creations to go to hell—but only so long as it remained an idea, so long as it was never put into practice. Why don't we make clear distinctions between ideas and practice? What makes us turn ideas into practice? Doesn't that inevitably plunge us into failure and despair? Aren't dreams enough in themselves? We'd go crazy if we asked each dream we have at night either to turn into reality or else. Has anyone ever been able to shoot a dream?

"Yes," I replied, "but not with rifles. It took spears. The Aztec emperor Montezuma summoned everyone who'd dreamed of the end of his empire and the arrival of the conquistadors and had them put to death . . ."

He looked at his watch. It was seven. Time to leave. He wasn't interested in the Aztecs, and Mexico seemed to him a protective wall topped with broken glass.

# XXVII

I'm sitting opposite my wife, Luisa Guzmán, in the spacious
living room of the house we shared for ten years in the cobblestoned neighborhood of San Angel. Each of us is holding
a glass of whiskey, each stares at the other and thinks
something, the same thing or something different from what
the other thinks. The glasses are heavy, rounded, their thick,
rippling bottoms like the eye of an octopus at the bottom of
the Sargasso Sea. She's also hugging her stuffed panda.

I look at her and tell myself we'll have to do something
that bears no resemblance to the rest of our lives. That's what
imagination is all about. But looking at her sitting opposite
me, imagining her as she imagines me, I prefer to be clear
and concise. During those years, Luisa Guzmán did not manage my social life (she was reclusive) or my financial life (she
was supremely indifferent to money). She encouraged my literary life; she was patient about my work as a writer and
reader. But what she did manage was my sexual life. Which

is to say, she put up no obstacles to it. She thought that by standing aside she was ensuring my next return to her. That's how it had always been.

In any case, sitting there watching her watch me, with all the burden of memory on our shoulders, I realized that each time she had been one step ahead of me. She could not conceive a fidelity that could withstand the success of my first book. At the age of twenty-nine, I attained a celebrity I myself didn't celebrate very much. If there's one thing I've always known, it's that literature is a long apprenticeship that is always open to imperfection when things go well, to perfection when things go badly, and to risk at all times—if we want to deserve what we write. I didn't believe the praise heaped on me, because I knew I was far from achieving the goals I imagined; I didn't believe the attacks either. I listened to the voices of my friends, and they encouraged me. I listened to my own voice, and all I heard was this: "Don't accept success. Don't repeat it superficially. Set yourself impossible challenges. It's better to fail by taking the high road than to triumph on the low road. Avoid security. Take chances."

I don't know when exactly in our relationship Luisa felt I needed more, needed something more but needed her as well—something that would be the erotic equivalent of literary risk. Or ambition. We laughed a lot when, a week after we fell in love, a very famous Mexican writer visited and berated her for preferring me to him. "I'm handsomer, more famous, and a better writer than your boyfriend."

Our astonishment was due, more than to anything else, to the great author's continuing his friendship with her and with me, undeterred. His delirious plea for her hand (or a change of hands) had failed, but his amiable smile never did. Nor did, and this we knew from the start, his limitless ambition—so genial, so well founded, even though he took a dim view of it—to achieve power and glory through writing. Luisa showed me (or confirmed me in the certainty) that it's better to be a human being than a glorious author. But at times being a person involves greater cruelty than the naïve promise of literary fame.

Now, as we sat opposite each other, there was no need to tell her I couldn't do without Diana Soren; hugging her stuffed panda, a glass of whiskey in her hand, she reproached me, without saying a word, for all the accumulated cruelty in our relationship and threw in my face the ease with which I used the mask of literary creation to disguise it. Her eyes told me: You're ceasing to be a person. As long as you were, I respected your love affairs. But I've just now realized you don't respect yourself. You don't respect the women you sleep with. You use them as a literary pretext. I refuse to go on being one.

"It's your fault. You should have drawn the line the first time I was with another woman."

"Tender and evil. How do you expect . . . ?"

"For years you've put up with my infidelities . . ."

"Excuse me. I can't compete anymore with all these imaginative efforts and the fantasy of all the women in the world . . ."

"By maintaining our love, we ended up killing it—you're right . . ."

She hurled the glass, heavy as an ashtray, at me, hitting my lower lip. I gave the melancholy panda a melancholy look, stood up, rubbing my painful lip, and left forever.

# XXVIII

I didn't find Mario Moya. He was at a conference on population growth in Bucharest and wouldn't be back for two weeks. I shrugged and hoped the matter could wait. That was more or less the amount of time it would take to finish filming in Santiago. Then all of us would go back to . . . Where would Diana go? Where would I go? Would we stay together? I doubted it. Her husband was waiting for her in Paris. In Los Angeles, a Black Panther whom she talked to on the telephone at three in the morning. In Jeffersontown, Iowa, an idealized lost boyfriend, a midwestern Tristan who by now, perhaps, was a potbellied pharmacist, swollen with Miller beer, a fanatical Chicago Cubs fan.

I had no illusions. She wouldn't go along with me to some idyllic ivy-covered American campus. What I didn't want was for anything to interrupt present time, our time together in Santiago and later, with a little luck, a few days in Mexico City, a rendezvous in Paris . . . I did have illusions of our spending a summer together on Mallorca, an island we both adored, where I had recently spent time exploring with a marvelous friend, the writer Hélène Cixous, and where Diana and Ivan had a house . . .

Anything, I told myself on the flight back to Durango, anything but losing her for these last two weeks. One possibility came to my mind incessantly, excluding all others. I was her lover because they would not allow her real lover, the leader of the Black Panthers, to enter Mexico. Should I anticipate her rebuff, the break between us? Should I be the one to take the initiative and break with her before she, going even further, abandoned me, left, and forgot everything we were?

I had called her a few times from the capital. I have a hard time communicating by telephone. The invisibility of the person I'm talking to fills me with impatience and anguish. I can't match the words with the facial expression. I can't know if the person talking to me is alone or with someone, dressed or naked, made-up or clean-faced. The more technology advances, the more we compensate for our moral or imaginative deficiency with the only weapon available: lies. I've just stepped out of the shower. I'm naked. I'm just walking out the door. I'm sorry. I'm alone. I'm alone. I'm alone.

"I love you, Diana."

"Words are very pretty and don't cost much."

"I miss you."

"And yet you aren't here. Well, well."

"I'll be back on Friday. We'll spend the weekend together."

"I'm dying of impatience. 'Bye."

I didn't have time to tell her that I was afraid for her,

that she should watch out, that it was for that reason I'd gone to the capital, to try to find something out and protect her. But my relations with the Díaz Ordaz government were terrible. I had only one friend in it, my schoolmate Mario Moya, Undersecretary of Internal Affairs, and he was away.

"I came here for your sake, Diana. I'm here because of you," I would have wanted to shout to her, but I was uncertain about things. There was no hurry, I told myself. I was much more concerned now with knowing what her expression had been when she spoke so abruptly to me. Would that be the next technological advance—a telephone with a screen so we can see the face of the person speaking to us? What an atrocious violation of our privacy, I told myself, what infinite complications: always being ready, hair combed, makeup fresh, dressed (or undressed, depending). Or quickly messing up one's hair to justify one's drowsiness: "You woke me up, darling. I was sleeping—alone." And a paunchy, bearded guy in a T-shirt next to her, watching football on television and chugging a mug of beer.

I began to be haunted by the idea that Diana was a work of art that had to be destroyed to be possessed. In sex, as in art, interrupted pleasure is a poison, but it also stimulates an ambiguity that is the amniotic fluid of both passion and art. Could I come out of this ecstasy at the cost of destroying Diana, the object that caused it? Should I, in other words, anticipate her? Should I ensure the possibility of continued pleasure in its unique atmosphere of ambiguity, of might-have-been or might-have-not-been, nothing resolved, everything in the marvelous realm of the possible, where alternatives, for a story or for a passion, multiply and open like a fan that compromises but enriches our freedom?

I landed in Santiago at five in the afternoon, still unable to answer my own questions.

The ride from the airport to Diana's house seemed especially long this time. The tedium of the town, its stores closing and their metal gates crashing down like deafening waterfalls of steel, was broken only by the swish of the trees and the growing shadow of the mountain, which dominated the city. I saw nervous turkeys and scarred cactus fences covered with the markings of lovers—names (Agapito loves Cordelia), linked hearts—mortal wounds that left dark scars on the green flesh.

"What's going on?" I asked the cabdriver. "Why are we going so slowly?"

"It's a demonstration. Another student protest. Why don't they spend their time studying? Bunch of lazy bastards."

The town square smelled of mustard. A vague, depressing cloud covered it. People ran for the side streets, coughing, covering their noses with handkerchiefs, sweaters, newspapers. I imagined the governor barking behind a window. I saw the young leader Carlos Ortiz run by, blood pouring down his face.

"Close your window, señor, and hold on."

He made a U-turn and escaped toward the neighborhood where my temporary home, my papers, and my books were. I felt the landscape of Santiago falling to pieces, its inhabitants rapidly losing their features . . .

# XXIX

The expression on Azucena's face told me something was up. She never showed anything, and I knew nothing of her emotions. Sometimes we chatted, very cordially, as I've said. We were linked by language—lines of poetry we all learned in Spanish-language schools: "Yesterday's gone. Tomorrow hasn't arrived."

I respected her, as I've also said, for her dignity, her pride in doing well what it had fallen to her to do well in this world. In the little world of Hollywood transplanted to Santiago, she was the only one, in the end, who was neither sorry for herself nor devoured by a desire to rise in the world. She was superior to her mistress. She didn't want to be someone else. She was someone else. She was herself.

Now she received me in a dimly lit, strangely silent house. She had an unaccustomed grimace on her face, and it took me a while to find in it any sympathy, any affection, any solidarity with the other Hispanic person present. For a moment I felt perfectly melodramatic, like the poet Rodolfo asking his Bohemian companions why they're walking around so silent, why they're weeping. Mimí is dead. Azucena was holding back, unintentionally of course, something like a death announcement.

"Diana?" I asked, as I might have asked out loud, except that now I said her name almost in a whisper, as if I were afraid of interrupting a novena to the Virgin.

"Wait here. She's on her way," said Azucena, inviting me to stay in the living room.

Night was falling. Lew Cooper wasn't there as he usually was, standing at the liquor cabinet mixing a cocktail justified by the hard work involved in exterior shots. The bedroom door was closed. But my clothes were there and, in the bathroom, my Italian toothpaste. Impatiently, angry, I walked to the corner where my typewriter, my papers, and my books were laid out. Someone had imposed order on everything. Everything was arranged in perfectly symmetrical piles.

I went back to find Azucena, to protest this violation of my creativity. Instead, I found Diana, divided by the light of the gallery at nightfall, half light, half shadow, perfectly cut in two, like one of Ingres's female portraits, my beloved Diana Soren. She walked toward me, separated from herself by the light, yielding not an inch of her luminous person to her dark person, or vice versa. The contrast was such that even her short blond hair seemed white on the side of the gallery window and black on the wall side. The charm was broken by her outfit. In a pink quilted robe buttoned to her throat, totally domestic, and a pair of fluffy slippers, Diana Soren looked like an upside-down mushroom, a walking thumbtack . . .

It wasn't that—not the magic of her appearing between light and shadow, not how absurd I instinctively judged her appearance to be—which kept me from walking over to her, embracing her, and kissing her as I'd always done. She never reached me. She stopped and sat down in a rattan chair, the most imperial object in this house devoid of pretensions, and she stared at me intently. I sat down in the thatch-backed chair opposite my desk and crossed my arms over my chest. Perhaps Diana had read my mind. Perhaps she imagined, as I did, how our love would end and what would follow it. It occurred to me to tell her, before saying anything else, how useless my trip to Mexico City had been. I found out nothing about the FBI threat General Cedillo had hinted at. I was going to tell her, but she spoke first, quickly, brutally.

"Forgive me. I have another lover."

I controlled my confusion, my rage, my curiosity . . .

"In the U.S.?" I asked without daring to mention my telephone indiscretions.

"Another man is living here."

"Who?" I asked, not daring now to think about The Return of Clint Eastwood and telling myself that at least they wouldn't allow a Black Panther to cross the border. The stuntman? I laughed at myself for even thinking it. I laughed even more at the ludicrous possibility of old Lew Cooper's sleeping in my bed, next to Diana.

"Carlos Ortiz."

"Carlos Ortiz?"

"The student. You saw him here in Santiago. He says that he knows you and admires you and that he's spoken with you."

"Suppose he hated me and refused to speak with me." I tried to smile.

"Excuse me?"

"This isn't about excuses. It's about talking things over."

"I don't like explaining myself."

I stood up, enraged. "I just mean talking."

"We can talk if you like."

"Why, Diana? I thought we were very happy."

"We also knew it would end."

"But not like this, suddenly, prematurely, before the filming was over, and with a boy—"

"Younger than I am?"

"No, that doesn't matter."

"Well, what does? The fact that I hurt you, humiliated you—do you think I like doing that?"

"Not having carried our love to its end, not having used it up completely, that—"

"I don't think there's anything left."

"Diana, I offered you everything I could—to go on being together if that's what you wanted, to go together to some university," I said stupidly, confused by a sudden vague feeling of sentimental blindness.

She was right to answer me like this, brutally, without sentiment. "Don't be naïve. Do you really think I'd waste my life in some shitty hick town covered with ivy but made of nothing? You must be crazy."

"Why crazy? You've been running away from another hick town, and you never want to give yourself the opportunity, the chance to go home and then leave again, be renewed."

"Darling, you're delirious. I felt suffocated in that town. I would have left there no matter what."

Gently I asked her to explain. I think she sensed how I felt, because she added something I liked. She said I shouldn't misunderstand her, that in Jeffersontown she felt suffocated not only by its smallness but by the immensity of the nature surrounding it. It was a world she couldn't grasp.

176

And in the world you did choose, I asked her, do you feel protected? Will you ever know who you are, Diana? You have to be protected by other people, by the sect, by the beautiful people, the jet set, the Black Panthers, the revolutionaries—anyone, as long as there's noise, weeping, joy, commotion, belonging. That's what you want, that's what I don't give you, because I'm stuck in a corner writing for hours at a time?

I was making a fool of myself. I'd lost control. I was falling into everything I hated. I deserved Diana's response.

"I know who I am."

"No, you don't!" I shouted. "That's your problem. I heard you talking with that black man on the telephone. You want to be someone else, you want to absorb the suffering of others so you can be another person. You think no one suffers more than a black person. When are you going to learn, you fool, that suffering is universal, even white?"

"Carlos is teaching me all about it."

"Carlos?" I said it like an echo not only of my own voice but of my own soul, incapable of telling Diana that I'd just seen him, injured, in a demonstration in Santiago.

"It's in your books," Diana said coldly.

"Did he tell you that?"

"No, I read them. I thought you were a real revolutionary. Someone who puts his actions where he puts his words. It's not true. You write, but you do nothing. You're like an American liberal."

"You're crazy. You don't understand anything. Creation is an action, the only action. You don't have to die in order to imagine death. You don't have to be imprisoned in order to describe what a prison's like. And if you get shot or murdered, you're useless. You don't write any more books."

"Che went out to be killed."

"He was a martyr, a hero. A writer is something much more modest, Diana." I kept on talking to her, exasperated but now, possibly, in control of my arguments.

"Carlos would climb a mountain to fight. You wouldn't."

"So what's that got to do with you? You're going to follow him? Going to be the warrior's woman?"

"No. His base is here. He fights here. He'd never follow me."

"That makes things work out fine for you, right? Knowing that poor kid won't follow you. Unless he gives up the guerrilla business and becomes a gigolo. Poor Diana. You want to be someone else? Do you want to be the midwife of universal revolution? Do you want the role of Joan of Arc married to Malcolm X? Let me tell you something. Try to be a good actress. That's your problem, sweetheart. You're a mediocre, bland actress, and you want to compensate for your mediocrity with all the furies of your real-life person. Why don't you really work at the roles you get in movies? Why do you reject them and take on characters you've only heard talked about?"

"You don't understand a thing. I've already had you."

"One month three weeks and four days."

"No, I know you through and through. I know who you are. I should have known from the first instant, but I let myself be dragged along by the fantasy that you were different—action and thought, like Malraux . . ."

"For God's sake, spare me these revolting comparisons . . ."

"Naïve. All you can offer me is decency. Naïve. Decent. And cultured!"

"All defects of the worst kind . . ."

178

"No, I admire your culture. Really. A solid base, no doubt about it. Very solid. Classic, man, classic."

"Thank you."

"On the other hand, the boy . . ." She spoke with a ferocity I'd never seen in her, a hallucinatory savagery, as if finally she was showing me the dark side of the moon. "Everything about him is wrong. He smells bad, he's got rotten teeth, he needs to see a dentist, his manners are awful, he's got no refinement at all, he's rough, I'm afraid he's going to beat me up—and because of all that I like him, because of all that I find him irresistible. Now I need a man I don't like, a man who'll bring me back to the gutter, the sewer, who'll make me feel I'm nobody, who'll make me fight again, work my way up, feel I don't have anything, that I have to earn everything, who'll make my adrenaline flow . . ."

I ran to embrace her. I couldn't hold back anymore. She was crying and she clung tightly to me, but she didn't stop talking between sobs. "You're crazy. I'm not looking for a black or a guerrilla, I'm looking for someone who's not like you. I hate people like you, decent and cultured. I don't want a famous author, decent, refined, Western no matter how Mexican he thinks he is, European like my husband. You're my husband all over again, a repetition of Ivan Gravet, the same thing all over again. It bores me, it bores me, it bores me. At least my husband fought in a war, ran away from Russia, persecuted for being a Jew, for being a boy, for being poor. You, what have you ever run away from? What's ever threatened you? Your table's always been set, and you've always been chasing after me, trying to catch me, to catch my imagination . . . You're my husband all over again, except that Ivan Gravet is more famous, more European, more cultured, more refined, and a better writer than you!"

She stopped for air, swallowing her tears. "I can't stand men like you."

She twisted out of my arms. She turned her back to me and walked to the liquor cabinet. I followed. She mixed a drink with trembling hands. She spoke to me with her back turned.

"I'm sorry. I didn't want to hurt you."

"Have a drink, it'll make you feel better. Don't worry," I said, putting my hand on her shoulder. A mistake.

"No. Don't touch me."

"I'm going to miss you. I'm going to cry over you."

"I won't cry over you." She gave me a final look, the synthesis of all her looks—happy eyes, tired eyes, bedazzled eyes, lonely eyes, fugitive eyes, orphan eyes, remembering eyes, altruistic eyes, convent eyes, whorehouse eyes, fortunate eyes, unfortunate eyes, dead eyes.

She blinked several times in a strange, dreamlike, almost insane way, and said this: "Don't cry over me. Ten years from now your *gamine* will be an old lady over forty. What are you going to do with a lark with a fat ass and short legs? Thank God you're getting out in time. Count your blessings and cut your losses. Good-bye. *Désolé.*"

"*Désolé.*"

Azucena helped me pack my things. She took my clothes out of the bedroom. I asked her with a look if the student was there. We understood each other without having to speak. She shook her head. She didn't have to help me—she did it out of pure goodwill, so I wouldn't feel alone, cuckolded, thrown out, or, in the last instance, badly thought of by her. She also knew I didn't need her help; I made her understand how thankful I was for it. We exchanged few

180

words while we packed my books, papers, and pens into my two briefcases. Then I carefully covered my typewriter.

"She was a beginner, too. She likes to help people just starting out."

I laughed. "The midwife of the revolution, that's what I told her."

"She's a very unhappy person. Seriously. She feels persecuted."

"I think she's right. Sometimes I thought it was nothing but paranoia. I'm beginning to think she's right. The boy's only going to complicate her life."

"Diana likes risks. You didn't give her that."

"So she told me. Tell her to watch out. I couldn't do anything for her in Mexico City. I hope she gets a lot out of her new love."

Azucena sighed. "A beautiful woman doesn't look for beauty in her partner."

It seemed a cruel remark coming from her. I imagined the roles reversed. Azucena and a handsome man. The equation was unfair. Once again, the man was the winner. Never the woman.

In the hall, I ran into Lew Cooper. He didn't say anything to me. He just grunted.

Azucena ran out into the street after me and handed me something.

"You forgot this."

It was a marmalade jar full of hairs.

# XXX

Jealousy kills love, but it leaves desire intact. That's the real punishment for betrayed passion. You hate the woman who broke the love pact, but you still desire her because her betrayal was the proof of her passion. That was the case with Diana. We didn't end in indifference. She had the intelligence to insult me, to humiliate me, to attack me savagely so I wouldn't resign myself to forgetting her, so I would go on desiring her with what we call jealousy, that perverse term for erotic will.

I saw the Santiago house for the last time in the growing darkness of a February afternoon. Now it was an impregnable fortress. That house I walked in and out of as if I owned it, where I wrote every day, was now alien and repugnant to me. I wanted to besiege it the way the Romans besieged Numantia in Spain, to burn it and destroy it the way the legions burned and destroyed the Jews' Masada. It was with that desire that I gave it a farewell glance, that I circled it one last time, as if instead of penetrating Diana I could penetrate the house we shared.

Fate had given me that woman. No man could take her away from me. Least of all someone I considered a coreligionist, a left-wing student, a traitor . . . The fetid smell of tear gas drifted in from the center of town, and at that moment I wished that the army had captured my rival, that General Cedillo personally had cut off his balls, and that if he escaped I might one day find him and have the courage to kill him myself. As I thought about it, though, I was gripped by an amusing irony: "Don't deprive the government of that pleasure."

Norman Mailer says jealousy is a portrait gallery of which the jealous man is the curator. I summoned up the images of each and every one of my moments with Diana, but now with the young student in my place, in my positions, enjoying what had been mine, filling his mouth with the taste of peaches, enjoying the limitless wisdom of Diana's caresses, transformed into the sole spectator of the lake in which the Huntress is reflected . . .

Jealousy is like a life within our lives. We can catch a plane, go back to the capital, call up friends, begin writing again, but all the time we're living another life, apart although within ourselves, with its own laws. That life inside our lives manifests itself physically. There's a battle in our guts. We wake up, and it's Omaha Beach at Normandy in our stomachs. True. A savage, bitter, bilious tide swirls, rises, and falls from our heart to our guts and from our guts to our worn-out, useless sex, a war casualty. It makes you feel like pinning a Purple Heart on your dick. And then a funeral wreath. But the tide doesn't celebrate anything and doesn't stay in one part of the body for very long. It runs through it like a poi-

183

sonous liquid, and its objective is not to destroy your body but to besiege it and squeeze it so its worst juices rise to your head, stick like hard green serpent scales on your tongue, on your breath, in your eyes . . .

For a moment, the break made me feel expelled from life. The way you feel when someone you love dies. But we can show that pain. The dark, poisoned pain of jealousy must be hidden, to avoid both compassion and ridicule. Exposed jealousy exposes us to the laughter of others. It's like returning to adolescence, that unfortunate age in which everything we do in public—walk, talk, look—may be the object of someone else's laughter. Adolescence and jealousy separate us from life, keep us from living it.

The curious thing about this experience of mine was that I felt separated from life, not out of adolescent fear of the ridiculous but because of the fatal sadness of age. Diana made me feel old for the first time. I was forty-one. My rival couldn't be more than twenty-four. Diana was thirty-two. I laughed. Once in Italy I tried to get into a discotheque with an eighteen-year-old American girl. The man at the door stopped me, saying, "It's only for young people." To which I replied, with a straight face, "I'm her daddy."

I was thirty-five then. How many doors would be closing on me now, one after another? She said that she was doing it for my own good. In ten years, she'd be barrel-assed and flabby. I was sorry I hadn't said no, that she could be someone else—she wanted that anyway—if she gave herself over to her profession, if she stopped looking for roles that would give meaning to her life outside the movies . . . Thinking that over, I tried to convince myself of my superiority. All I had to do was to work seriously on my own stuff: I wouldn't get old in ten or even a hundred years. That was the power of literature.

But on the condition that we share that power with others. And I, as I said, felt I'd fallen from my initial power, and in that I was like Diana. My literary anointment, like her Saint Joan, was long past. The aura of the beginning was fading, dying. How do you rekindle the flame?

I returned from Santiago with a handful of useless pages. All I had to do was read them coldly, as a counterpoint to my burning internal convulsion, to realize they were no good. I would publish them anyway. They had a political purpose. But if no one read them, what political purpose would they serve? I was willfully fooling myself. I needed to lie to myself as a creator in order to survive as a man. But at the center of my unquiet desire, one conviction shone with a brilliance that grew day by day. The writer's *other* is not there, big as life, waiting for what he hopes he'll be given. The *reader* must be invented by the *author, imagined,* so that he reads what the author *must* write, not what it is expected he will write. Where is that reader? Hidden? Let's find him. Unborn? We must wait patiently for him to be born. Writer, toss your bottle into the sea, be confident, don't break your word— your words—of honor even if today no one reads them. Wait, desire, desire, even if no one loves you . . .

I could never have said this to Diana Soren. Something melodramatic and pointless would have come out, like "There are great roles for mature actresses." It would have been pointless because at that moment in her life Diana So- ren wouldn't have known what to do with her own success.

I realized that and loved her more than ever. I loved her all over again. Thinking that saved me from my ardor, from my interrupted way of living, from my break and expulsion from life, from my life within my life but separated from my life. That is, it saved me from my jealousy. I saw her, with the little distance I'd managed to win, as a woman who really did know who she was. A foreigner wherever she was, condemned to solitude and exile. A political activist, condemned this time to despair, irrelevance, and finally, again, solitude. A mature actress condemned to decadence, oblivion, and forever, again, solitude. The story of Diana Soren is the story of her solitudes. Diana was the goddess who hunts alone.

Did she and I share that? I could formulate only one answer. I would have given everything for her, only because she wouldn't have given anything for me.

Accepting that truth was how I distanced myself once and for all from Diana, renouncing all my romantic illusions of getting back together with her or spending time together . . . Perhaps only one link remained between us. We could tell a story to all those who've wanted to free themselves from a love relationship without hurting anybody. It's impossible.

I thought about Luisa. My jealousy of Diana consumed me even as my love for Diana was dying. I wanted to give that love to Luisa. With her I felt no jealousy at all—she could be the receiver of a love I no longer wanted to waste on my game of mirrors, on the anxiety of all these combinations . . . I was fooling myself yet again.

It's true that once more she accepted the rules of our pact. There was no weakness or submission in it, just active strength. Our pact survived all minor accidents. We had a house, a daughter, a group of friends, everything that makes possible the daily life which with Diana was impossible.

I said I was fooling myself. Other irresistible temptations would come. Foreign actresses get bored when they're on location. They want company without risk. They pass names around among themselves: in India, Tom; in Japan, Dick; in Mexico, Harry. Gentlemen who will take you out, who are well mannered, handsome, intelligent, good to be seen with, good lovers, discreet . . . How could anyone resist the parade of beauties who formed this information circuit to which, to my eternal joy, I belonged at the age of forty-one? How could I deny myself the game of mirrors in which were reflected image within image within image, passion and jealousy, desire and love, youth and old age, the pact of love and the pact with the devil: Push back my Judgment Day, let me enjoy my youth, my sex, my jealousy, my desires for one more day . . . but also let me enjoy my pact with Luisa. Why not hope that death, or separation, is a long way off?

She didn't fool herself. "He'll always come back to me," she would tell our friends. She knew that beneath that incessant tide a sediment of necessary stability was amassed, in which love and desire united without violence, discarding the need for jealousy to increase desire, or the need for guilt as thanks for love. Luisa waited patiently behind her incredibly beautiful mestizo mask for the inevitable day when one woman would give me everything I needed. Just one. She wasn't that woman.

Diana went away. She went when the rainy season began in Mexico and the air once again turned to crystal and gold for a single day.

# XXXI

I read about one part of Diana Soren's final drama in the
newspapers.

When Diana left Mexico, she was pregnant. I didn't know
it, but the FBI did. With that information, they decided to
destroy her. Why? Because she was an emblematic figure of
Hollywood radical chic, the celebrity who lends her fame and
gives her money to radical causes. When I met her, Diana
supported the Black Panthers. I've already mentioned the relationship I found out about at night and by telephone. I
knew every shade of her support. The FBI doesn't deal in
subtleties.

I want to imagine that the the "general public" in the
United States did differentiate between, say, the integration-
ist policy of a Martin Luther King and the separatist policy
of Malcolm X. I think that during the years I'm talking about
many white Americans (many friends of mine) supported
King's nonviolent civil protest as a progressive ideal: the grad-

ual integration of black people into the society of white America, the conquest by blacks of the privileges of whites. Malcolm X, however, advocated a separate, black nation opposed to the white world because it only knew and accepted injustice. If the white world was unjust with itself, how could it not be unjust with the black world? Both, in any case, would live in ghettos separated by color but united in pain, violence, drugs, and misery.

Those irreconcilable options needed a bridge. In Paris, Diana met James Baldwin, who shared at least two things with her: exile as solitude and the search for another, fraternal American. Baldwin, who stood between the two extremes, was a source of perpetual doubt; he deliberately muddied the waters so that no one would believe in easy justice or the inevitability of racial injustice, two faces of the same coin. Baldwin did not want humiliating, charitable integration. Nor did he want the union of black with black to be the chain of hatred toward whites. What Baldwin asked of whites and blacks, Southerners and Northerners, was the simplest and most difficult thing: Treat us like human beings. That's all.

"Look at me," Baldwin told Diana. "Look at me and ask yourself about the life, hopes, and universal humanity hidden behind my dark skin . . ."

Judging by Diana's nocturnal conversations, I imagined she thought the same. She wanted to be uncompromising about racism and white hypocrisy, but she wanted to be equally uncompromising in her opposition to a black world radically separate from the white world. The explanation seems to me, having known her, quite clear. Diana Soren wanted to see herself as someone else in order to see herself as she was. She took the risk of seeing blacks only as she wanted to see them, and she paid dearly for it.

The FBI, like the KGB, the CIA, the Gestapo, or Pinochet's DINA, needs to simplify the world so as to designate the enemy clearly and annihilate him without a second thought. Political police agencies, the guardians of the modern world and its well-being, always need a reliable enemy to justify their jobs, their budgets, their children's daily bread.

In Washington, it was decided that Diana Soren was the ideal candidate for that role. Famous, beautiful, white, the Saint Joan of radical causes (I called her the midwife of revolutionaries without imagining that my metaphor would be a reality in the cruelest way, Diana was placed under surveillance and invisibly, silently harassed by the FBI. The Bureau was waiting for the right moment to destroy her. It was merely a matter of opportunity. Diana Soren was destructible. More than anyone. She believed that injustice was fought not only with politics but with sex, with love, and from the romantic depths which made her ideally vulnerable. When the Bureau learned of Diana's pregnancy—while she was still in Mexico or soon thereafter—they realized it was time to move against her, to take advantage of her weakness.

It was then I understood General Agustín Cedillo's warnings and cursed myself for not having found Mario Moya in Mexico, for not believing Diana, for treating her with contempt ("You're paranoid") and locking myself in the prison of my jealousy. But really, what could I have done? It was already much too late when I found out what was going on. Was I the father? I don't think so—we'd taken precautions. Was the father young Carlos Ortiz, my successor in Diana's favors? That was more likely. She saw him as a revolutionary hero, while I was a tedious repetition of her own husband.

Still, a Mexican revolutionary does not have enough symbolic force to provoke the puritanical democratic white general public of the U.S.A. It would have been like having a baby with Marlon Brando—Viva Zapata!—an exotic experience, yet one that could readily be assimilated. But that the fair, blond star with blue (or were they gray?) eyes, descendant of Swedish immigrants, born in a small Midwestern town, brought up with soda fountains and Mickey Rooney movies, a Lutheran, a graduate of the local high school, the sweetheart of the football team and, one time, of a strong, healthy boy, a girl favored of the gods, chosen from among eighteen thousand hopefuls to play a saint; a rich, free woman married to a famous man, darling of the jet set—that this favorite of the white God would descend to the depths of miscegenation, to the murky, dark surrender of her Caucasian femininity to a brutal black penis, disturbed the night of the American soul, revived the bloody phantoms of castration, of blacks hung with their testicles in their mouths, of burning crosses, of the Klan galloping on . . .

A mulatto was only acceptable, imaginable, as the son of a white man and a black woman, the result of the whim or despair of the plantation owner, the white master too respectful of his white wife, the white master with the feudal right to spend the first night of marriage with the black bride, the white master enervated by his white wife's long pregnancy, the father of the mulattoes: a white patriarch . . .

But that a white woman might be the matriarch of the light-brown world, might populate the forests of the New World, the American utopia, with degraded mestizo bastards—no, that repelled even the most liberal conscience, that went to the very center of the Yankee heart, stirred up the guts and balls of Yankee decency. The child had to be black, the offspring of a black revolutionary and a frivolous, crazed white actress. If not, it would mean total horror. The white woman was the slave of the black.

The FBI is patient. It waited until Diana's pregnancy was obvious. Approval of the defamation plan went along these lines: Diana Soren has provided financial support to the Black Panther Party and must be neutralized. Her current pregnancy by [name blacked out] gives us the opportunity to do so.

The Bureau proceeded in the following manner. Agents planted a rumor with Hollywood's gossip columnists. They circulated a letter signed by a fictitious person: "I've been thinking about you, and I remembered that I owe you a favor. Imagine, I was in Paris last week and by accident I ran into Diana Soren, so pregnant she's as big as a house . . . At first I thought she'd gotten back together with Ivan, but she told me that the father is [name blacked out] of the Black Panthers. That girl sure gets around, as you can see. In any case, I wanted to give you first shot at this one . . ."

Hollywood gossip columns began to repeat the rumor: "The top item in today's news is that Miss D., the famous actress, is expecting. The proud papa is supposed to be a prominent Black Panther." The news spread, scaled the heights of credulity, won more converts than the Bible, and was consecrated in an American news weekly with a world-wide circulation—in fact, it is so well distributed that it was one of the two magazines you could get at the drugstore in the Santiago town square, the place where I'd gone to buy toothpaste and where a young student approached me with an invitation to speak to his group . . .

"Excuse me," I said then (I laugh at myself today), "but

I don't want to compromise my North American friends. I'm their guest."

The magazine was the first to mention Diana's name. She and Ivan sued them for libel and won something like ten thousand dollars.

The next thing I learned was that Diana had given birth prematurely by cesarean section and that the baby had died after three days.

The next week she flew from Paris to Jeffersontown to bury it. She displayed the body in a funeral parlor. The entire town marched around the coffin, eager to verify the color of the baby's skin.

"It isn't white."

"It's not black, either. The features aren't black."

"You can never tell with a mulatto. They're tricky."

"How can you know if this is really Diana's baby? A black fetus is the easiest thing to throw in the garbage."

"Do you mean she bought the body of a white baby just to bring it here for us to see?"

"How much would that cost?"

"Is it legal?"

"You look at that baby carefully. It's white."

"But with a touch of the tar brush. Don't kid yourself."

"So who's the father?"

"Her husband says he is . . ."

That sent the line of curious spectators into waves of laughter.

Diana Soren paid no attention. She was too busy taking photos of the tiny body in the white coffin. She took 180 photographs of the dead child.

# XXXII

At the end of the 1970s, I met Ivan Gravet in Holland. We'd both been invited to spend a long weekend in the country at the castle of our mutual friend Gabriella van Zuylen. Gabriella is a charming, very beautiful woman, a lover of gardens and a friend of Russell Page, the magnificent British park designer, about whom she wrote a monograph.

The castle is an impressive pile, especially because in Holland's flat landscape it stands out like a mountain. Gabriella has dedicated herself to extending, completing, and beautifying the tranquil, bovine Dutch landscape with the mystery of nature as conceived by the baroque imagination—contrived, varied, circular.

Among the curiosities of her garden was a labyrinth of very high hedges whose perfectly geometrical form, as regular as a botanical spiral, could only be appreciated fully from the roof of the castle. But if you were inside the maze, you quickly lost any sense of its form, and lost your way as well. Sooner or later, Gabriella's thirty guests all explored the maze and all got lost until she came to our rescue, laughing.

My wife, who's afraid of spaces without exits, refused to go in the maze and went off with Gabriella to the Frans Hals Museum in Haarlem. I ventured in, willfully desiring to get lost. First of all, I wanted to play along with the maze's intention. Secondly, I was convinced that to enter the maze with the goal of getting out was obviously how you'd become the prisoner of the mythic bull who inhabits it. But if you got lost, losing the will to survive, it would please the Minotaur, make him your ally, allay his suspicions. That's how Theseus should have proceeded.

I did not have Ariadne's thread. But when I suddenly found myself face-to-face with Ivan Gravet inside the maze, I decided that Diana Soren was the thread on which, in a certain way, both of us were relying at that moment—only at that moment. I'd seen him, of course, since Friday, at Gabriella's magnificent dinners and lunches. At night, we were supposed to wear evening clothes, and Ivan was the sole exception, wearing a jacket I can only compare to those I saw in photos of Stalin or Mao: a gray tunic with very long sleeves, buttoned to the neck and worn without a tie. It wasn't what was then called—during an attack of Third World fashion— a Mao or Nehru jacket. Ivan Gravet's tunic looked as if it had either been bought in the GUM store in Red Square or been handed on from some member of the Politburo. The last time I'd seen one like it was in a photograph of the justly forgotten Malenkov. Khrushchev wore only suits and ties. In Ivan Gravet's outfit—which he didn't change the whole three nights we spent at the castle—there was nostalgia for a lost Russian world; there was humor, but there was also mourning . . .

We laughed when we met. We couldn't have spoken any

other way, said Ivan. Why? I asked; I've never said anything, no one would connect us. We're in another country, I added brutally, and besides, the wench is dead. I was curious to know more, but I also wanted to force Ivan to react within the brief time we had in the maze. How strange: I felt that both of us ascribed less importance and devoted less time to this labyrinth, created to capture forever those who venture into it, than we did to going through customs at an airport.

"It's that you didn't know the difficulty of loving a woman you can't help, change, or leave," he said.

I agreed. Diana was part of a past that no longer concerned me. For eight years, I'd been living with my new wife, a healthy, modern, active, beautiful, and independent woman. We had two children and a loving sex life in which we treated each other with respect without submitting to each other, aware that the continuity of our relationship depended on our never taking it as something certain, customary, given, with no effort on our part.

Far from Diana, far from my past, I still felt close to the literary joy I'd recovered. I did not burn the pages I'd written in Santiago with Diana at my side, but I had leapt from them, with more strength and conviction than ever, to the work that was waiting for me, that summoned me, and that gave me the greatest happiness in my life. I hadn't wanted to finish writing it. No novel gave me so many intelligent readers, readers who were close to me, who were permanent, who mattered to me . . . With that novel, I found my real readers, those whom I wanted to create, discover, keep. Those who, like me, wanted to discover the figure of greatest essential insecurity— not worn-out psychologies but helpless figures developing at another level of communication and discourse: language, history, epochs, absences, nonexistences as characters, and the novel as the meeting place of times and beings that would never otherwise encounter one another.

Ivan Gravet answered me affectionately. He was not offended by my little quotation from Marlowe's *Jew of Malta*. We were writers and men of the world. I had to understand two things about Diana's fate. Diana and he had never protested the FBI's lies, never succumbed to a surge of the racism in their Caucasian genes. There had been no doubt that the FBI had played that card. To protest the libel could have been taken as disgust for or rejection of a black baby. They, Diana and Ivan, saw the trap. But Diana's anger was directed against the political manipulation of her sex. The FBI had reduced her to a sex object. It had presented her as a white woman hungry for a black man. Besides, finally, it was untrue. The father wasn't black—as he and I know well. Nor was the baby.

"Did she have to exhibit it in Jeffersontown? I didn't think public opinion there mattered to her."

"It did. She never wanted to be judged as a schizoid personality—the small-town girl split between home, family, spiritual peace, middle-class stability, Christmas and Thanksgiving, and all the rest . . ."

"Did she have to photograph the child's body? It seems to me a—"

"She had to be the witness to her own death. That's all. She wanted to see how she would be seen if she came back to her town dead. She wanted to see the faces, hear the comments while she still could. That baby was a substitute Diana. See? The wench died in her own country. And she dies all the time."

"Forgive me. *Je suis désolé*," I said and remembered Diana.

He squeezed my arm. "She wanted to respond to oppression with something more than politics, which she didn't understand. She thought sexuality and the romantic life would be her contribution to a world filled with both. She didn't realize that one thing leads to another. You know? Rebellion leads to sexual excess, which leads to alcohol, alcohol to drugs, drugs to terror, to violence, to madness . . ."

"Then she will have to be judged just as she didn't want to be judged—as the small-town girl who couldn't resist the evil of a world she was unprepared for . . ."

"No. I loved her. Excuse me: I still love her."

"I don't anymore."

"She was politically naïve. I warned her many times that democratic governments know that the best way to control a revolutionary movement is to create it. Instead of embodying it, the way totalitarian regimes do, they invent and control it and thus have an enemy they can count on. She never understood that. Again and again, she fell into the trap. The FBI decided to finish her off with a huge laugh."

"I thought you were going to defend her."

"Of course. Dear friend, Diana Soren was an ideal being. She epitomized the idealism of her generation, but she was incapable of overcoming a corrupt society and an immoral government. That's all. Think of her that way."

We heard the happy voice of Gabriella calling for us in the maze, summoning us in to lunch . . .

# XXXIII

It was Azucena who told me the most terrible version of Diana's end. I ran into her quite by chance on the Ramblas in Barcelona sometime in the mid-1980s. I was visiting my friend and literary agent Carmen Balcells on a mission of mercy. I wanted to ask her to support the Ecuadoran novelist Marcelo Chiriboga, unjustly overlooked by everyone but José Donoso and me. He had a minor post in the Foreign Ministry in Quito, where the altitude was suffocating him and the work left him no time to write. What could we do for him?

Seeing Azucena reminded me of the days we'd spent in Mexico and the pleasant experience of her always dignified presence. As we walked toward Paseo de Gracia, where I was staying, she spoke with her head lowered, giving a grim, objective account of the events, which, out of respect for Diana and herself, she did not want to cheapen with sentimentalism.

Azucena went to the United States with Diana for the

baby's funeral in Jeffersontown. On the flight from Paris to New York and then on to Iowa, Diana was calm, with a distant, almost beatific smile on her face, imagining the body in the white coffin that was with her on this trip, a trip she'd made dozens of times before. But on the return flight, from JFK to De Gaulle, something horrible happened. Diana excused herself to go to the lavatory. Three minutes later, she came screaming and running down the aisle, naked. No one dared to touch or stop her until a powerful black man intervened. He wrapped her in a blanket and returned her, suddenly calm but staring intently at the man's eyes, to her seat next to Azucena in first class. Azucena gave her some sleeping pills and assured the stewardesses that Diana would sleep for the rest of the flight.

She stayed quietly in Paris for some time, sharing the apartment on Boulevard Raspail with Ivan, whom she no longer had relations with. She preferred to pick up boys in bars and hotels, especially hippies with a spiritual air and a dedication to drugs, which she then began, of course, to use seriously, as if they were the next step in her spiritual maturation and her rebellion. But she also belonged to an alcohol culture, and Diana was not a woman who would abandon an earlier phase in her life when she was diving into a new one.

From what Azucena told me, I came to understand an important truth about my old, momentary lover. She loved everything, but not greedily or egoistically. On the contrary, she loved things as a form of generosity toward herself but also toward the world or worlds she was living in. The provincial world of the Midwest and Hollywood, the intellectual world her husband offered her in Paris, the rebellion of the 1960s, liberal causes, the Black Panthers, the Mexican revolutionary—she collected all these worlds so they would go on

200

being hers, but, most of all, so that none would consider her an ingrate, unable to take responsibility for her past. The past was an unfulfilled obligation that she had to bear, even if she failed.

"Is that why she wouldn't sacrifice anything? Is that why she went back to Iowa with the dead baby?"

"I don't know," Azucena said simply. "The truth is that Diana suffered greatly. She would get in trouble and never get out except by getting in more trouble."

She wanted to stay thin so she could go back to movies. Quick diets made her weak and strained her nerves. To quiet her fears, she would drink more. The alcohol would make her fat. So she'd use more drugs to get thin and stop drinking. She was in and out of one clinic after another. In one, she would dedicate herself to repeating again and again the simplest gestures and tasks. Azucena would visit her every day and see her get up, go to the bathroom, urinate, defecate, eat her breakfast, wash her clothing in the sink, straighten her bed, and climb back in it. But each of those acts, each one, would take two to three hours and wear her out. After sweeping the room, she would sleep till the next morning, when she'd get up, go to the bathroom, and begin the round all over again.

She would stare at Azucena during these times, with a mixture of attitudes and emotions. She would watch her out of the corner of her eye to make sure that Azucena was looking at her, that she was aware of what she was doing, and, most important, that she was approving, applauding her effort and the importance of each one of her actions . . .

For a long time she stayed in a sanatorium near Paris, overlooking the river. All one could see from her window was factory chimneys. There, Diana set about rediscovering her face, tracing it with her hand in the mirror, as if she were trying to remember herself. That act became a daily ritual. The permanence of her features seemed to depend on it. Without that ritual, Diana would have lost her own face.

One day, though, Azucena noticed that Diana's fingers no longer followed the shape of her face. Instead—Azucena saw it by coming closer—they drew something else over it. She didn't want to alarm her. Curious, she observed her for several days, concerned, trying to figure it out. With her finger, the woman was drawing over her face the exterior landscape of the chimneys. She wanted the world. She wanted to create it. She could reproduce it only as an invisible tattoo on her face in a misted-over mirror.

Inside, she was dead. Her interior death preceded her exterior death. The men she was with were, at best, her guards, her jailers. They also used drugs. She saw them as friends one day, enemies the next. She'd run away from them to pick up total strangers outside the hotels near the big train stations—the Gare de Lyon, Austerlitz, the Gare du Nord. The stations for anonymous businessmen, traveling light. Who were they? That was the point: no one. Sex without baggage, nothing that would truly enter her life, because she let nothing go and excess baggage was very heavy and very expensive . . .

"She simplified her life so much that at the end she was only eating dog food."

No one would give her work. She imagined a strange movie—Azucena told me that afternoon in Barcelona, sitting in a café on the Ramblas—in which nothing happened but in which everything happened at the same time. There were four simultaneous scenes, with no people, just places, colors, sensations. One place was a desert. That was Mexico. Another place was pure stone. That was Paris. Another place was

202

lights—many, many lights. That was Los Angeles. Another place was snow and night. That was Iowa. She wanted to bring them together in a film, and only then, when all of them were joined, would she enter the picture.

"Know something, Azucena? Now I'm going to go back and see for the last time each one of the places where I've lived."

That was the last thing Diana said to her.

# XXXIV

Toward the end of the 1970s, I ran into Diana in a Paris restaurant. She smiled at me fixedly but didn't recognize me. She was like a dead woman whose eyes hadn't been closed. Her smile was meant for no one in particular. Her stare was out of phase with the objects before it. A zombie with swollen flesh. A miserable body. A malnourished beauty. I had a useless feeling that I couldn't keep from overwhelming me. Might I have helped her? Was I in some way guilty for what I was seeing and what was looking at me without recognizing me? Would only a Midwestern boy have made her happy forever? Is there a part of life that won't let itself be purified? I have no explanation for the inexplicable. But neither does the world.

# XXXV

A few years later, I took a nonstop flight from Los Angeles to New York. I had just given a series of lectures at some California colleges and decided to reward myself with the luxury of a first-class seat on a jumbo jet so I could sprawl out comfortably for the six-and-a-half-hour flight. There were very few people in first class. After we were all seated, an airline official escorted a splendid woman to the first row. She passed in a cloud of perfume that conjured both Olympus and the jungle: a black woman in a short skirt, with long legs, perfect thighs, marvelous breasts, but a maternal belly, the belly of a goddess of the subjugated earth of Africa and America. Her tensed neck emblematized and betrayed all the cares, fears, and timidity of this lioness, which is what she was, crowned with an animal mane the colors of a sunflower—copper, red, blond, black, pubic.

Of course I knew who it was: Tina Turner. What I noticed was her pain, her modesty, which dissipated any air of stardom, any undeserved arrogance. Her veiled eyes said to themselves, I have no right to all this, but I deserve it. She didn't apologize for her fame, but she preferred that we share, at least in the anonymity of travel, the human meaning of her songs. She snuggled up next to the window, took off her shoes, and put on her sunglasses; a gracious stewardess covered her with a vicuna blanket—soft, infinitely swaddling, maternal, protecting the singer from the sound and the fury, caressing her with the sweet drowsiness of fatigue.

I didn't want to stare at her too much; I didn't want to be curious or impertinent. I thought of the song Diana Soren listened to so often—"Who Takes Care of Me?"—and, looking at the sleeping lioness wrapped in her own skin, I admired, with painful tenderness, the strength of this humiliated, beaten, cheated-on woman who overcame her troubles without taking revenge on her tormentors. Without asking for the death or the imprisonment of anyone, earning, on her own, the right to be herself and to change the world with her voice, her body, and her soul, without sacrificing any of the three. Her art, her race, her spirit . . . Poor Diana, so strong that she had no defense against the weaknesses of the world. Marvelous Tina, so weak she learned to defend herself against all the powers of the world . . .

# XXXVI

I went to Iowa only many years later, while on a lecture tour in the Midwest. Whenever she'd ask me, "Help me re-create my hometown," I would tell her I couldn't: "I have nothing to do with that." "You've seen it in movies," she said, teasing me for my amateur cinematographic erudition. That's why I know—I retorted—that the small town in the movies is always the same small town. It's been there at M-G-M since time immemorial, the town where Mickey Rooney captivated all the girls in high school and put on plays in the barn. Main Street with its signs: barbershop, soda fountain, Woolworth's, the local newspaper, the church, and the town hall standing in for the saloon and whorehouse of the heroic era. I told her that all that stuff she and I believed in was invented by Jewish immigrants from Eastern Europe who, out of gratitude, wanted to construct an ideal image of the United States as perpetually bucolic, peaceful, innocent. A place where boys on bicycles delivered newspapers, where sweethearts held hands on porch swings, and where the universe was an immense perfectly mowed lawn, perfectly open and limited only, perhaps, by that white fence Tom Sawyer painted.

When my friends from the University of Wisconsin took me to Iowa in 1985, I discovered that the myth was real, although it was impossible to know if the town had imitated Hollywood or if Hollywood was more realistic than we thought. The courthouse, a neo-Hellenic building with cornices and blindfolded statues guarding the steps of justice, presided over life in Jeffersontown. Main Street was exactly what I expected: low buildings on each side, shoe stores, drugstores, a Kentucky Fried Chicken with the ubiquitous Colonel Sanders, a McDonald's, and a bar.

"The high school. Don't leave out the high school," she would say.

"But I've never been there. I've got nothing to do with that. How do you expect . . . ?"

The boys still meet to drink beer in the tavern. They're tall and strong. They talk about what they did that Saturday when I was in Diana's hometown. They went out to hunt raccoons. It was the young men's favorite sport. That carnivore, native to North America, has a difficult Algonquin name, *arahkun*, and a prodigious nocturnal life. Its fur is grayish-yellow, its tail has black rings on it, it has small erect ears and almost human hands, thin as those of a pianist. But its face is a black Venetian mask that disguises it so it can climb trees more easily. It's omnivorous, but it washes everything before eating it, and, disguise on top of disguise, it makes its den in hollow trees. Masked raccoon: it sleeps in winter but doesn't really hibernate. It delivers its litter, of up to half a dozen little raccoons, in only sixty days. Young, it's pleasant and playful; old, it's as irascible as a solitary grand-

208

father. It eats everything—eggs, corn, melons. It's the scourge of the local farmers, who hunt it down. The fiery old ones know how to escape, but the young ones fall more easily. Young or old, however, they turn fierce when cornered. In the water, they're dangerous—they can drown their enemies.

The raccoon abounds in the hills, bluffs, and plains of Iowa, a state of fertile black soil, of immense pasturelands that have been composting for millions of years. The boys spent the week working at tasks that were sometimes pleasant, sometimes disagreeable. Math is too abstract, geography too concrete, too alien. Who cares where Mexico is, or Senegal or Manchuria? Who lives there? Does anyone live there? Sure: dagos, chinks, kikes, niggers, and spicks. Have you ever seen anyone from there? The drugstore, on the other hand, is the place for dates; love begins over a shared cherry Coke with two straws, as in the Andy Hardy films, and continues at the movies on Saturday night, when sweaty hands are linked in love and popcorn is consumed while on the screen the lovers see themselves live as they are in their seats, looking at Mickey Rooney and Ann Rutherford holding hands, looking at two imaginary kids holding hands, looking at . . .

"There'd be basketball games at the gym. Don't miss them. They're easy to imagine. They never change."

History class was the most boring. It always took place "before," in a kind of eternal museum where everything was dead, where there were no people like them except when they were translated to the screen and turned into Clark Gable and Vivien Leigh. That was history, even if it was a lie. Reality could be an illusion—drinking a chocolate malted with your girlfriend, going to the movie to see a new illusion each week. They all knew they'd get married right there and would live right there, and since most of them were good boys, they'd be good husbands, good fathers, and would resign themselves to the aging of their girlfriends—too much flaccid flesh, the death of sex, the death of romance, romance, romance, like the moon going dark forever.

On the other hand, a group of young men hunting raccoons vibrates with a single emotion, like nothing else. Their rifles were obvious extensions of their masculinity, and they showed them, cleaned them, loaded them as if they were showing one another their phalluses, as if acts barely insinuated in the locker room were authorized in the raccoon hunt by those rifles so easy to buy in a country where the right to keep and bear arms is sacred—it's in the Constitution.

"Go back to the high school for a minute, please . . ."

It was as if the dogs were blind, their huge floppy ears given over to their single sense, smell. Blind, deaf, plagued with blue ticks, which the boys would amuse themselves by pulling off after hunting and a few beers around the fire.

"It's a building from the fifties, modern, low . . ."

Sometimes, when they lost the scent, the dogs would wander off, blind, deaf. All one had to do then was to leave the owner's jacket out on the plain, and the dog would invariably return. This was the real world. This was the admirable, fixed, concrete, intelligible world. In which a dog would come back to the spot where his owner's jacket was. The boys hugged one another, laughing and drinking, elbowing one another in the ribs the same way they snapped towels at one another in the locker room, scrupulously refusing to look too low. The rifles were enough; you could stare at a rifle. You could touch your buddy's rifle. Together, they could skin raccoons around the fire and go back to town with their bloody trophies and their deaf dogs.

"There's an auditorium in one wing of the building . . . You have to visit it."

One of the boys was different. Hunting raccoons and skinning seemed pointless to him. People used to go to football games in raccoon coats. No more. Hunters in the Wild West used to make themselves raccoon caps. No more. Once upon a time, there were men here, real men. You had to be a real man to hunt what there used to be in Iowa. Buffalo, nothing less.

"He gave me a nickel with a buffalo on one side and an Indian on the other. I still have it. He told me to take care of it, it was rare. First the buffalo disappeared, then the Indians, and then the coin with their picture. Now on one side there is a distinguished gentleman, the untouchable American saint Thomas Jefferson, and on the other his house, Monticello."

Who killed the last buffalo? that boy asked Diana. This land was full of buffalo. Who, who killed the last one . . . ?

In the United States, telephone poles are now metal. Here, they are still made from trees. It's as if the wires couldn't speak without the voices of the forest. The night I spent in Diana's town thinking about her was a dark night, and in my hotel room with the window open, I felt like one of those blind hunting dogs, blinded by the darkness; but even if I had no sense of smell, I did have my ears at the ready to hear what the silence was saying beyond the darkness. Would they talk about her? Would they remember how one day her father took her to the plane for Los Angeles, a seventeen-year-old girl with long chestnut hair, and how she came back one day in a Cadillac convertible, wrapped in a mink but with her hair cut short like an army recruit's, as blond as a . . . star? That's how they showed her off on Main Street, between the drugstore and the shoe store, the courthouse and the high school.

"Come to the auditorium. Wait till the moon comes up. Let's wait a while. You're going to lift my skirt. You're going to caress my mound. You're going to take off my panties. When the moon comes up, you're going to take my virginity."

She was the girl next door, same as the others except for those unique, incomparable gray eyes (or were they blue?). I don't know if those eyes of Diana's could live forever looking at themselves in the blue eyes of her parents, relatives, and friends. I looked at the eyes of the old people in Iowa, and once again I was surprised at the simplicity, the goodness, the recaptured, eternal childhood of those eyes, even when the hair above was white as Christmas and the faces as wrinkled as the map where the buffalo once roamed. Were these men, white and soft as marshmallows, the same cruel, insensitive boys who went out on Saturdays to hunt raccoons? Were they the same men who, full of blood lust and unsatisfied violence, went out to kill the last buffalo?

"Now, screw me now, when the moonlight comes through the skylight, screw me, Luke, screw me like the first time, give me the same pleasure, make me tremble the same way, my love, my love . . ."

When the moon came up that night in Iowa and I saw it from the window of the Howard Johnson's, I was convinced that Luke, wherever he was and whoever he was now, had cut it out and ordered it hung in the sky. In her honor. It was her paper moon.

The sun rose on the Sunday when I was to leave, and I remembered that she'd told me, Don't miss going to church and listening to the sermon.

212

Whenever I go to a Protestant church, I'm a bit afraid. It's not mine, and the absence of decoration makes me fear an essential hypocrisy that deprives God of His baroque glory and keeps the faithful from sharing it, all in exchange for a white Puritanism that is only painted white, like the sepulchers of the Pharisees, rendered white the better to cast the sins of the world on the rest, those who are different, the others.

The pastor ascended the pulpit, and I stupidly tried to give that role to a famous actor—Orson Welles in *Moby-Dick*, Spencer Tracy in *San Francisco*, Bing Crosby in *The Bells of Saint Mary's*, or Frank Sinatra in *The Miracle of the Bells*. I surprised myself by laughing softly as I remembered Hollywood's extravagant imagination in creating priests who were boxers, singers, or Falstaff types . . . No. This little man with white hair and a hatchet face was almost a human Host, colorless, as white as celestial flour.

It took me some time to perceive the carbonic heat of his eyes, like black marbles. And his voice did not seem to emanate from him; fascinated, I began to think his voice was only a conduit for another voice, distant, eternal, that described the Lutheran faith, that let us have radical confidence in God because God justifies man, God accepts man because man accepts that he is accepted despite his being unacceptable. How can man have faith in God's acceptance of all the sins that all individuals, even the cleanest, hide in their heart of hearts and excrete into the material world? Man, in faith, believes he is received by the grace of God and that his crimes are pardoned in the name of Christ, who with His death paid for all our sins. The price the church puts on such a faith is that of obeying within and without the will of God. That requires faith, not reason, because reason leads to despair. It's hard to conceive rationally that God justifies the unjust. The believer embraces the Gospel in order to understand that *gospel* means that *God justifies believers in the name of Christ, not in the name of their merits.* That is what you should understand perfectly this Sunday. You should believe that God pardons because He is just, not because you are. You will never be able to accumulate enough merit to be pardoned for torturing a fly or disdainfully stepping on an ant. You erroneously think God is just.

No, justice is not what God is but what God gives. What God grants. What you can never give to yourself or anyone else. Even if you are just, you cannot give justice to anyone except through God. Blasphemous people: imagine a God as unjust as you or as just as you would like to be. It doesn't matter—nothing matters, nothing, nothing. Only God can dispense justice, not you. Only God can impart the law, even if He himself violates it by creating you. Live with that, beloved flock, try to live with that conviction. Have the courage but also the anguish of knowing the truth about God: we receive justice; we do not have justice; justice is not given, justice is not deserved, justice is something that God gives us when He decides, because not even God Himself is just, God only has power, the power to pardon even though He himself deserves no pardon. How can He deserve it when He committed the error of creating the lustful, criminal, ungrateful, stupid, self-destructive beings that we all are, the creatures of a guilty God? Live with this, brothers and sisters. Have the strength to live with our impossible and demanding faith. Think about a God who deserves no forgiveness but who has the power to pardon us. Do not fall into despair. Hope, and be confident.

He finished. He smiled. He gave a laugh; he stifled it with a hand over his mouth.

After the service, I walked the streets of Jeffersontown, where Diana Soren was born and grew up. On the porches the old people rocked, with white hair and blue, innocent, always innocent eyes, so distant from geography and history, so innocent they didn't want to know what their leaders were doing in those unknown places full of spicks, dagos, niggers, and especially Communists. At nightfall the eyes of innocence look at a paper moon over a tiny town in Iowa and give free rein to Thomas Jefferson because he's white and elegant even if he has slaves. He's more intelligent than all of them together—that's why they elected him. We have only one president at a time; you've got to believe in him, put his profile on the mountains and the coins, toss the Indian-and-buffalo coins in the air: let's see where they fall. The earth is immense, black as a slave, rotten as a Communist, wet as a Mexican's back; the earth goes on growing, fructifying, because the earth's been putrefying for millions of years.

It was her paper moon, the same one that she saw, mythical symbol of her femininity, before going out into the world with a single arrow and a bow, Diana the solitary huntress over the black, rotten earth of Iowa. It was her paper moon, the same one that illuminated the last night of the buffalo, when the boys hunted them on horseback, firing their rifles until they shot out the moon itself. The same moon that allowed the angry raccoons to reach their dens in the tree hollows, chased by the boys who killed the last bison on the plains. But they hunt in a pack, all together, shouting, victoriously raising their phallic rifles under the moon. Only she hunts in solitude, waiting to be touched both by the rays of moonlight and by the compassion of the capricious, culpable God who created her.

I'm sure that, thinking about all this, the pastor smiled and might have wanted to laugh and laugh, to make a joke, to make a good impression, to exonerate himself of the anguish of his own sermon. But none of that mattered. That night the waters of the Mississippi, to the east, rose along with those of the Missouri, to the west, overflowing their tributaries and flooding the earth of Iowa from Osceola to Pottawattamie, from Winnebago to Appanoose; carrying away in its muddy stream houses and carriages, wooden posts and neo-Hellenic columns, church steeples, wheat and corn crops, potatoes with Cyclopean eyes and roosters with crests like imperial banners; erasing the tracks of buffalo and drowning the desperate raccoons; putting the inundated plain to sleep in order to return to the Indian name for the land. Iowa: sleeping land but land watched over by the antonym of the white nation. Iowa: hawkeye. Sleepy some moments, alert at others, the land sinks, disappears, and no one, as time passes, can go home to it again.

# XXXVII

Diana Soren is dead. She was found putrefying inside a Renault parked in a Paris alley. She'd been there for two weeks. She was wrapped in a Saltillo serape. Could it have been the one she bought with me in Santiago? The news article says that with her body there was an empty bottle of mineral water and a suicide note. The Paris police had to call the sanitation squad to decontaminate the dead end where they found her body locked up with death for two weeks. What was left of her was covered with cigarette burns. Even so, I wondered if finally, in death, she'd been comfortable in her own skin.

# XXXVIII

The FBI rendered Diana a posthumous homage. The Bureau admitted it had slandered her in 1970 as part of a counter-intelligence program called COINTELPRO. The director of the agency at the time, J. Edgar Hoover, approved the plan: Diana Soren was destroyed because she was destructible. In 1980, Acting Director William H. Webster declared that the days when the FBI used derogatory information to fight supporters of "unpopular causes" were gone forever. Calumny, he said, is no longer our business. Our only concern is criminal conduct.